Abigail

People of the Promise

Leah
1990

Joseph
1992

Hagar
1992

Esau
1993

Deborah
1993

Othniel
1994

Abigail

James R. Shott

HERALD PRESS
Scottdale, Pennsylvania
Waterloo, Ontario

Library of Congress Cataloging-in-Publication Data
Shott, James R., 1925-
    Abigail / by James R. Shott.
      p. cm. — (People of the promise ; 7)
    ISBN 0-8361-9030-0 (acid-free)
    1. Abigail (Biblical character—Fiction. 2. Bible. O.T.—History of
Biblical events—Fiction. 3. Israel—Kings and rulers—Drama.
4. David, King of Israel—Drama. 5. Women in the Bible—Fiction.
I. Title. II. Series: Shott, James R., 1925- People of the promise ; 7.
PS3569.H598A64 1996
813'.54—dc20   95-25415
                                                 CIP

The paper used in this publication is recycled and meets the minimum
requirements of American National Standard for Information Sciences
—Permanence of Paper for Printed Library Materials, ANSI Z39.48-
1984.

ABIGAIL
Copyright © 1996 by Herald Press, Scottdale, Pa. 15683
    Published simultaneously in Canada by Herald Press,
    Waterloo, Ont. N2L 6H7. All rights reserved
Library of Congress Catalog Number: 95-25415
International Standard Book Number: 0-8361-9030-0
Printed in the United States of America
Book design by Paula M. Johnson/Cover art by Jeff Legg

05 04 03 02 01 00 99 98 97 96 9 8 7 6 5 4 3 2 1

To my brothers,
John and Bill, who share
with me the proud heritage
of our family name.

1

"YOU ARE WELL NAMED, Nabal—you fool!" she exclaimed.

As soon as she said it, Abigail knew her husband would punish her. What happened was more sudden and vicious than she expected.

His fist lashed out at her face, striking her with all the drunken fury at his command. Jagged colors flashed before her eyes. The world spun around her. Then she opened her eyes and stared at the gray skies; she was flat on her back in the dust of the courtyard.

Her husband stood over her for a moment, swaying, probably wondering whether to continue beating her. Finally he shrugged, turned, and lurched over to the table, where he poured himself a cup of wine. He swilled it noisily, slopping some of it down his beard.

Abigail lay unmoving, not wanting to arouse his anger again. She felt no pain, although she was aware of a trickle of blood from her mouth. Nor did she feel fear. She had never been afraid of her husband.

They had been married two years; only once before had he beaten her. That was just a few days after their wedding. She had called him "Nabal" then, too. The name infuriated him, and he had struck her. She had never called him that since—until now.

Everybody called him Nabal—behind his back. To his

face they called him Kenaz ben Elah, a Calebite of the tribe of Judah. His grandfather, in fact, had been Caleb ben Jephunneh, the patriarch of Judah and companion of Joshua. But everyone—servants, nobles, tradesmen—knew him simply as Nabal, the Fool.

Abigail explored with her tongue the tiny cut on her lip where the blow had broken the skin against a tooth. Nothing serious. Not even painful. Maybe it looked worse than it was, which might explain why her husband had not continued the beating. The flagon of wine on the table was more attractive to him than beating his prostrate wife.

She continued to lie in the dust, watching him. He seemed to seek any excuse these days to drink heavily. Today it was the sheep shearing. "A festival," he called it. Anything for an excuse to swill his wine.

Then she gasped, as she recalled what had prompted her to call him Nabal. He had just bragged to her that he had sent the emissaries of the outlaw David away empty handed. He certainly was a fool. His rash actions would mean a raid by the savage outlaws and a brutal death for everyone.

The renegade David ben Jesse had made quite a reputation for himself among the landowners of Israel. Wherever he went, he raided. First he would send a representative to the landowner demanding tribute. A lot of tribute. Whole flocks, many donkeys, food, even servants. The intelligent landowners would pay up; the stupid ones refused—and suffered.

Kenaz was now draining his third cup. He had been drinking heavily all day, and certainly he should have reached his capacity by now. He hiccuped, belched loudly, and staggered off toward the largest building of his estate, where his sleeping quarters were located.

Now it was safe to try to get up.

"Oh, Mother Abigail, are you all right?"

Abigail looked up to see her young handmaid Shua hurrying toward her from the servants' house. Evidently she had remained hidden until Kenaz had gone.

"Yes, Shua."

Abigail's voice remained calm. In crisis situations she always kept her composure.

Shua knelt down in the dust beside her, reaching out her hand to offer what comfort she could.

"Oh, that beastly man! He's drunk again, Mother Abigail. That Nabal—"

"His name is Kenaz!" snapped Abigail. She sat up suddenly, ignoring the whirling of the courtyard around her.

"Yes, my lady."

Abigail smiled. Her servants called her "Mother Abigail" most of the time, even though she had never become a mother in the two years of her marriage. They called her "My Lady" when she scolded them. One was a term of affection; the other of respect.

Shua cupped her hand on Abigail's elbow to assist her, but her mistress shook it off and stood up alone.

"I'll take care of myself. You go find Jarib. Tell him I want to see him immediately."

"Are you sure you're all right, Mother Abigail?"

Again she smiled at being called Mother Abigail. For two years Shua had called her that, even though they were exactly the same age, seventeen. She hoped it was a sign of respect and affection. Nobody ever called Kenaz "Father Kenaz." Only Nabal.

Abigail pushed Shua away and went to the table, where she poured some water from a flask into a bowl. With the dampened sleeve of her dress she dabbed the side of her mouth, then washed it thoroughly in the water. She poured a cup of wine and swished it inside her mouth, feeling for the first time a sting of pain.

"Mother Abigail, are you all right?"

Jarib came bustling in from the servants' quarters where Shua had found him. He was an older man, his black beard streaked with gray, his crooked teeth stained. But he, like all the servants, had always shown genuine affection and respect for the mistress of the house.

Abigail was tired of people asking if she were all right. She turned to face him. "Jarib, we are in great danger. Now, here's what I want you to do. . . ."

Swiftly she gave her orders. Jarib was immediately to assemble a caravan of donkeys, carrying two hundred loaves of bread (which would almost clean out the bread cellar), two bushels of roasted grain, one hundred raisin cakes (the ones her husband had ordered prepared for the Shearing Festival), and two hundred figs.

"Be ready by sunup," she told him. "I want you to take them to the outlaw David. Choose whatever men you need to help you."

Jarib frowned, sucking his teeth. He opened his mouth to say something but closed it again. Then he shook his head, muttered "Yes, my lady," and turned to carry out his orders.

When Abigail had first come to live in Carmel after her marriage, the servants were respectful to her, but she did not dare to give orders. As time passed, however, her authority grew, and now even an older servant like Jarib, who had some standing in the household, obeyed her commands.

Still dabbing her mouth with the sleeve of her gown, Abigail went into the main house. The lamps had not been lighted yet, and the sun was sinking behind the western hills. She picked up a small oil lamp, adjusted the wick, and lit it from the brazier with a straw. Then she climbed the stairs to her husband's sleeping chamber.

The room was large and well ventilated, with windows on two sides of the room. The shutters were open; a cool breeze flowed through, bringing relief from the heat of the day. Before morning it would be cold, and Kenaz would never wake up long enough to pull up a blanket.

He had sprawled across his bed and lay on his back snoring, mouth open. He hadn't even bothered to take his sandals off. She knelt before him, unlaced his sandals and pulled them off, then raised his head to place a pillow under it. After draping a blanket over him, she left the room.

He would sleep all night and probably into the next morning. Then when he woke he would be too groggy and tormented by headache to care what she had done. Eventually he would have to be told, but by that time she would have turned aside David's savage anger and saved their household from destruction.

In the courtyard Abigail found Jarib supervising the gathering of food for the outlaw David. Three men were working with him, and she was glad to see that one was Hezro, a youth betrothed to Shua. His muscular arms shone with sweat as the moonlight flooded the open yard.

"Jarib," she called.

The older servant turned to face her. "Yes, Mother Abigail?"

"Will you be ready to leave before daylight?"

The man nodded his graying head. "There's not much left to do. I'll take these three men with me to manage the donkeys. Hezro says he knows where to find David."

"Is that true, Hezro?"

The youth put down the barrel of wine he carried so easily in his strong arms.

"Yes, Lady Abigail. I . . . er . . . have heard about his camp in the wilderness."

Abigail studied the handsome face of the muscular youth. His black eyes under the shock of curly black hair were clear and confident. She wondered why he hesitated when he spoke of the outlaw's hideout. Did he know more about David than he let on? She decided to press him to see how much he knew—or how much he would tell of what he knew.

"What kind of a man is this renegade David? Is he as savage as everybody says?"

Hezro smiled, his white teeth contrasting with the short growth of his youthful black beard.

"No, my lady. He's—that is, I have heard he is a good and gentle man."

"I see. Well, I hope so, because I'm going with you. I want to meet this renegade who has rebelled against the Lord's Anointed."

Hezro frowned. He opened his mouth to say something but closed it and instead turned aside. "Yes, my lady," he murmured, picked up the wine cask, and went about his work.

Abigail turned to the older servant.

"I need to talk to this 'gentle' outlaw. I'll be ready in the morning."

"No, Mother Abigail. You can't! This David, they say, is a lusty young man. You wouldn't be safe!"

"Nevertheless, I'm going. I must talk with him."

"But my lady—"

"Oh, let her go, old man!" Hezro had shouldered the wine barrel and was standing with body slightly bent under the heavy load. "No harm will come to her."

"How do you know, Hezro? Do you think you can protect her all by yourself?"

Hezro grinned, his face in the moonlight appearing young and boyish.

"Well, I know one thing. If I did, I'd get no help from you. You don't know the difference between a sword and a meat cleaver!"

"Why you impudent piece of trash! Someone should teach you a lesson!"

Abigail placed her hand on the old servant's arm.

"Let him speak, Jarib. I want to know why he thinks I will come to no harm."

Hezro swung the barrel of wine to the ground as easily as if it were empty. "My lady, he—I mean, they say he is particularly courteous to women. Maybe he is somewhat of a brute when it comes to dealing with men, but with women, children, and old people, he is gentle as can be."

"How do you know so much about him?"

The youth hesitated as he tried to decide how much to tell her. A jaunty tilt of his chin and a defiant look in his eyes told her he had reached a decision.

"My lady, ten of his men came to Nabal in the field today to ask him for help. They were very courteous, and—" He hesitated, frowning.

Abigail encouraged him. "And?"

"And one was my cousin. I had a chance to talk to him after Nabal turned them away."

She did not correct him for calling her husband "Nabal." Other matters were more pressing just now.

"I see." She stared at him thoughtfully. "And you have talked to your cousin before this, haven't you?"

"Er . . . yes, my lady. Several times. David's men have often been in our neighborhood."

Jarib interrupted. "They couldn't be. He would have attacked us."

"On the contrary, old man. They have never done us any harm. In fact, day and night they were like a wall of protection around us and our flocks. They have never stolen so much as one sheep."

"Maybe not." Jarib's sharp tone reflected his annoyance with the younger man's attitude. "But David is a rebel against the Lord's Anointed, and—"

"Let him speak, Jarib." Abigail was far more interested in Hezro's information now than Jarib's opinions.

She turned to the young servant. "And what did your cousin tell you today?"

Hezro grinned in his boyish way. "He said there's going to be a lot of trouble for our master and his family. Nabal is such a stubborn lout no one can even talk to him!"

Abigail wondered if the last statement was a quote from the cousin or an expression of Hezro's opinion. Probably both. Well, no time to do anything about that now. "Get on with your work. I'll see you in the morning at sunup." She turned abruptly and went into the house.

Before sunrise Abigail rose and dressed carefully in a clean new robe. She tumbled Shua out of bed to help her with her hair. The young servant brushed it carefully and braided it, fastening the braids to the top of her head. When she put on her tall headdress with the veil, Abigail knew she looked attractive. Would it impress the outlaw? Or would it arouse his passion, so that he would—

She forced her mind away from that thought, taking comfort in the memory of what Hezro had said about David's gentleness toward women.

Jarib and his men were in the courtyard when she came out into the dusky morning. The old servant was whispering in a conspiratorial voice with Hezro and another servant. Abigail was just able to hear his last comment.

". . . and when she drops too far behind, I'm sure she'll turn back—" Just then he caught sight of Abigail in the doorway and hurried over to her, forehead wrinkled with worry.

"Mother Abigail, please don't go. It isn't safe."

"Is my donkey ready?"

"Yes, my lady, but—"

"Well, where is it?"

Jarib sighed and nodded toward the gate. The donkey tied there, with a bright blue blanket thrown over its back, was an old beast, gentle but slow. She wished they had readied one of the younger donkeys for her, but she made no objection. She was not a good rider, and this old fellow was not only gentle but broad of back. A long journey like this on a sharp-backed beast would be uncomfortable.

She smiled grimly to herself. She could guess why Jarib insisted on this grandfather donkey. She couldn't keep up with them, and finally she would grow discouraged and turn back. She set her mouth firmly. She would go on, no matter what. She had to talk to David.

"Go ahead," she said loudly so that all could hear. "I'll follow behind you."

The newly risen sun shone on her face as they crossed the valley heading toward the eastern hills. The chill of the night vanished in the refreshing warmth of the new day. It might have been an enjoyable excursion if she were going to visit a friend or picnic with Shua. But she was going toward the camp of the barbaric outlaw David, and her enjoyment of the morning was mixed with dread of what this day might bring.

What she knew of David was a mixture of rumor and servant's gossip. Also her husband Kenaz had spoken of him often, derisively, of course. The rebel had once been a favorite of King Saul, and even his champion in battle. But recently the young man had turned against the Lord's Anointed, leading a rebellion and seeking to usurp the throne for himself.

According to the stories, he had set up camp in the wilderness, where he attracted a fierce band of young warriors. Six hundred men, rumor said. Not quite enough to challenge the king in open battle, but enough to raid small villages and wealthy herdsman such as Kenaz.

She had heard Shua speak kindly of the outlaw, but Shua was betrothed to Hezro and had probably been influenced by him. Strange that Hezro would think of David as being gentle, even protective, toward Kenaz and his flocks. But no longer. Not after what Nabal had said to him yesterday.

Nabal! She must not think of him by that name. He was Kenaz, her lawful husband. Her father had betrothed her to him when she was only four and had been pleased to find her such a good marriage. At fifteen, she had become the mistress of a very prosperous household, even if her husband was a—

She shook her head sadly, trying to drive out of her mind such disloyal thoughts. She did not allow the servants to speak of him disrespectfully, nor would she allow herself.

She tapped her donkey with her stick. This grandfather beast was so slow! Already the others were far ahead of her. Jarib knew this would happen. In fact, as she thought about entering the mountains alone, she almost did turn back. But she clenched her teeth. Never! She would foil that sly servant's strategy.

She had no trouble following their trail here on the broad valley of Kenaz's grazing land. But when they left the plain and entered the rugged mountains, it would be more difficult. She again tapped her donkey, willing him to move faster.

She saw with dismay that Jarib and the others had entered the pass in the hills so far ahead of her that she would never catch up. She pressed her lips tightly together. Jarib—but she softened her thoughts toward her servant. The old man was doing this out of love for her. He meant well. But he was not wise enough to see that she must talk to David, in spite of his legendary brutality. Jarib would never be able to talk to David persuasively enough to convince him not to attack her household. Maybe Hezro could, however. He was an intelligent young man, but so young! No, only she could turn aside the fury of the outlaw, while running a desperate risk that he would not harm her.

Abigail had no time for more thoughts, however. As she urged her ancient donkey into the mountain pass, she concentrated on guiding it around the rocks, thornbushes, ravines, and soft sand. She must watch for snakes, although it was a little too early in the day for them to be out yet. They never appeared on the rocks until the sun was high overhead, and they could bask in the heat.

When she came to a fork in the trail, she didn't know what to do. There were no signs of the others, no trail left for her to follow. Had they turned off before this? No, she spotted a hoofprint going off toward the right. She would follow that trail and hope for the best.

She had not gone very far, however, before realizing she was on the wrong track. The road was too rugged for a mule train. She would have to go back. No, she wouldn't. The trail led in the right direction. Eventually she would come to a ridge and be able to see far enough ahead to spot the others.

The ravine she followed was narrow, its walls rugged with rocks and thornbushes. The old donkey picked its way carefully among the stones and bushes. Just ahead was a ridge she would have to cross. Maybe from the top—

Voices!

She heard someone speaking, then a laugh. Good. She must have caught up with her servants. She tapped the donkey, and he plodded forward carefully, wondering probably why its rider was so foolish as to travel on such a disgusting highway.

The voices grew louder. She heard several people laugh. But how could that be? There were only four of her servants, and they would not be coming toward her. Nor would they be laughing. Was it someone else?

At the top of the ridge appeared a group of men. They

wore swords and carried spears. Their skirts were bound up between their legs in the manner of fighting men. Who were they?

Suddenly she knew. They were a band of warriors, savage outlaws, led by the young man at their head, the one with light brown flowing hair and short beard. The one laughing at something one of his men had just said. She knew who he was.

2

ABIGAIL'S THROAT constricted. Her hand froze on the small stick she carried to prod the grandfather donkey. She glanced around, but her servants were nowhere in sight. She was alone. Alone to face the outlaw David.

She took a deep breath and slid down from the back of her mount. Her knees were unsteady, and she braced herself by placing a hand firmly on the donkey's back.

David had stopped suddenly, his hand reaching for the sword at his side. The men behind him, who had been laughing and talking, were now silent. The only sound intruding on this frozen moment was a snort from the donkey at Abigail's side.

The man she saw not ten paces away, standing in the center of the ravine, was of average height. His hair and beard shone with the oil he had brushed into it, reflecting his daily grooming habits. The hair color was a lighter brown than that of most Israelites.

So young! He was just a boy. He should be tending his father's sheep, instead of leading a large band of young men in the wilderness, preying on wealthy landowners, waging a desperate war against the anointed king of Israel.

But this was no weak boy. He stood straight, shoulders back, head up. He was a commander of men.

And a ruthless killer.

Abigail's hand pressed down on the back of the donkey. The startled beast shied away from her, leaving her standing alone. She had to do something.

She went to her knees and bowed low before him. "My lord David!" Her voice quavered slightly, and she struggled to control it. "I bring you gifts, and I beg you to listen to what I have to say."

Her voice sounded weak in the silence of the ravine. She wished she could take the words back, because she didn't want to appear as a beggar. But she had said them, and they could not be recalled.

She looked up to see the reaction on the face of the young outlaw leader.

He was grinning. "You bring me gifts, do you? All I see is an ancient donkey. I'll never get rich with gifts like this!"

The men around him relaxed, seeing no larger threat than a lone woman and an old donkey. Some laughed. They too were young, their beards as short as their leader's. They too had the fierce outdoor look of men who lived a wilderness life. She could only see about twenty of them, but there must be more just over the ridge.

One of the young men, a fierce warrior with curly brown hair and beard, spoke boldly. "Maybe the gift she's talking about is not that old donkey."

This brought a loud whoop of laughter from the men.

Abigail felt her face burning as the meaning of the crude youth's remark burst upon her. She set her jaw firmly as she rose to her feet. "My lord David," she said, anger giving her voice a firmness it did not have before. "Do not misunderstand me. When my servants arrive, you will see the gifts I bring you."

The laughter died away. Obviously they heard the rebuke in her words. She wondered if boldness were the better course of action before these savage men, but she didn't care. The man's crude remark had stung her.

"My lady, who are you?" David's brow wrinkled as he stared at her. "And what is your gift?"

She took a breath. "I am Abigail bath Kenaz of Carmel. I believe your mission is to kill my husband."

She was aware of gasps from the men behind David. She ignored them and concentrated on their young leader. He frowned but continued to stare gravely at her.

"Nabal's wife," said David

"Kenaz's wife," replied Abigail.

"Do you know," he said, his words slow and deliberate, "that I have sworn a sacred oath before Yahweh that before this day is over, not one male in your husband's household will be alive?"

The words were meant to humble her, but they caused an opposite reaction.

"In that case, sir," she replied with words as slow and deliberate as his own, "I am glad I'm not a man, or I would now be dead. I ask you, however, to spare the grandfather donkey, because I have no other means of transportation, and it's a long walk home."

The startled intake of breath from the men gave her a small measure of satisfaction. David continued to stare at her, as though assessing her with his eyes.

Whatever he was about to reply was interrupted by a shout from behind them. The ridge where the ravine rose to disappear into a canyon was filled with David's men, and they parted now as a new group of young men pushed through them. One seemed to be the leader. He was squat, curly-haired, and bearded, with bushy black eyebrows.

"David," he spoke boldly in guttural tones. "Look who I found while on patrol in the next ravine."

David had turned to look up at the man on the ridge. "Who's that, Joab?"

The man called Joab stepped aside to let the newcomer approach.

Abigail gasped. It was Hezro, her servant!

The young man walked confidently forward. "Greetings, my lord David!"

"Greetings to you, Hezro of Carmel. What brings you here today?"

Before the young servant could reply, Abigail spoke. "What is the meaning of this, Hezro?"

Hezro stopped and turned toward his mistress. The grin faded from his face. "Er . . . Mother Abigail, I . . . have met my lord David before. You see, my cousin—"

"And who is your cousin?" Abigail's tone was deliberately imperial as she looked around the men surrounding her.

One of the men stepped forward, the same man who had made the insulting remark a moment before. He grinned rudely. "I am, my dear lady." He bowed mockingly. "I am Shammah ben Agee, and I am Hezro's cousin."

She remembered, then, Hezro's claim that his information about David had come from his cousin, member of the outlaw band. She took an instant dislike to this fierce youth with his insulting manner and crude sense of humor.

Abigail turned back to Hezro. "I see that you know David. Are you too a member of this . . . these men?"

Hezro's youthful face reflected his confusion.

Before he could speak, Abigail turned to David. "My lord David, in keeping with your vow before Yahweh, you must kill my servant Hezro before this day is over."

She spoke impetuously, and she immediately regretted it. Her manner and tone of voice must sound sharp and shrewish, and her words were intended as an insult to David. She suddenly saw herself as she must look in David's eyes. He was a savage outlaw, she reminded herself, and could easily take offense. She bit her lip, telling herself to tread lightly, be more humble.

David, who had been studying her gravely before Hezro's arrival, now turned to her with amusement. His eyes sparkled, and his mouth slowly widened in a small grin. "Aha!" He began to stroke his bearded chin with his thumb and forefinger. "Our grand lady demands that we kill her servant and spare her donkey. She must have learned this sense of values from her husband!"·

Abigail knew then that the first impression she had made on David had been unfortunate. She must turn this around, become humble, if she wanted to save her household from destruction.

"My lord David—"

She was interrupted by a commotion behind the men on the ridge. They parted for a new arrival. Jarib! The older servant led one of the donkeys with the pack containing her gifts, followed by the other servants leading their donkeys.

"My lord David," she continued, raising her voice above the babble of surprise greeting these newcomers. "These are the gifts I bring you: two hundred loaves of bread, two barrels of wine, five dressed sheep, two bushels of roasted grain, one hundred raisin cakes, and two hundred fig cakes. And all I ask is that you listen carefully to what I have to say to you."

David's eyebrows raised as he stared at her. He did not even turn his head to look at the donkeys bearing the rich gifts. He only continued to rub his bearded chin with his thumb and forefinger.

Abruptly he dropped his hand, lifted his head, and spoke loudly, without taking his eyes off her. "Joab, take charge of these gifts." Then more softly he added, "I will listen to you, Abigail bath Kenaz. Come with me."

He strode forward, took her arm, and marched with her down the ravine. Thirty paces. Then, out of hearing range from his men, he turned to Abigail.

"Speak, my lady. I am listening."

"Er . . . my lord David. . . ."

Although she had planned what to say to him, she was still caught off guard. There was something disconcerting about this man who stood before her, looking at her so intensely. He was so handsome—but that wasn't what bothered her. She had dealt with good-looking men before, and it had not affected her as much as this man did.

No, it was something else. Some elusive quality. A combination of things. Boyishness—she wanted to mother him, protect him, instruct him. His steady gaze on her—she felt he liked her, even admired her, and she wanted to do nothing to change this opinion. And his humility—she had to remind herself that he was a leader of men. But he was so . . . so . . . childlike!

She also had to remember why she was there—to protect her husband, to preserve her household, to stop this personable young boy from becoming a murdering brute. What she had to say now, she had to say right.

He still gazed at her, and the silence between them had grown into minutes.

She had to speak. "My lord David. Please don't harm my husband. For my sake."

"And why shouldn't I? Didn't he refuse to help me do Yahweh's work? Is he not a fool?"

Abigail nodded. "Yes. I . . . I must admit that he is well named: Nabal. So often he embarrasses us and puts us in a difficult position because of his folly. But . . . please . . . forgive him. You are too big a man to soil your hands with his foolish blood."

He did not reply. Instead, his left hand went to his chin, and he stroked his beard again.

She continued. "You sent your men to us for a gift of food and supplies. That request has been met. Killing my husband and destroying our household is unnecessary."

He still said nothing. But his stare was disquieting. With difficulty she forced her mind back to what she had planned to say.

Something David said a moment ago came back to her. "You said you are doing Yahweh's work. If you are fighting his battles, and he really is on your side, then you are as safe under his protection as if you were living in Yahweh's pocket! You don't need to sling your stones at unimportant householders like my husband; trust Yahweh to take care of people like him."

She noticed that his mouth had opened, and he stared at her with a look of utter amazement.

Then the words seemed to pour out of her mouth. "My lord David, think of your future. Years from now, when you have attained all your dreams, you can look back on this moment. What will you say then? That you killed a small landowner and all the males on his property, just because you were angry at the way he insulted you? Or . . . that you graciously spared a fool and trusted your God to do justice?"

Her self-confidence left her in a rush. She had just blurted bold words to an outlaw who had rebelled against Yahweh's Anointed. Why had she spoken thus? Was it because he looked so childish and innocent, and she wanted to mother him?

She bowed her head.

"I . . . I'm sorry. Please forgive me for being so forward. I didn't mean . . . I'm sorry. . . ."

A moment of silence followed as she gazed on the ground. Then suddenly she raised her head with a jerk as he shouted, "Blessed be Yahweh, God of Israel, who has sent you to me this day!"

She gaped at him. His face glowed as he stared up into the sky.

He spoke again, this time not in a shout, but in a voice

softened as though in prayer. "Thank you, God, for speaking wisdom through the voice of this woman. You have prevented me from murdering a man and taking vengeance into my own hands."

He reached out and took both her hands in his. "Go in peace, dear lady. I accept your gifts . . . and your words. You may be sure I won't harm your husband or anyone in your household this day or any day."

When he smiled on her, it was like a benediction. She felt a warmth in her breast she had never experienced before.

Only later, as she rode home on her grandfather donkey, did a strange thought strike her. David, the boyish leader of the outlaw band, was so much a child that she felt a mother's love for him. And yet she was younger than he. And a thought disturbed her. *Is it really only a mother's love I feel for this young man?*

3

"WHERE HAVE you been, woman?"

Kenaz was drunk again. Celebrating the sheep-shearing festival. Celebrating alone.

"Where are the raisin cakes?" he demanded. "And where are those two barrels of wine I've been saving for this festival? You've been gone all day. Nobody knows where, or at least they won't tell me. But you'd better tell me. Tell me now. Where have you been?"

Abigail slid from the grandfather donkey and allowed Jarib to lead it away toward the stables. She frowned. Should she tell him now? No. Not in his condition. She would wait until morning.

If he would wait.

"My husband," she said, bowing her head before him. "I would like to prepare a full meal for you, to help you celebrate your festival. A kid, roasted and spiced the way you like it. And a date-nut pudding. I'll have Shua go to the garden for some fresh leeks, and then—"

"Well, do it. Hurry. What are you standing there for? After I've eaten, you will tell me where you were today."

"Of course. Now why don't you go lie down while I prepare the feast?"

As Kenaz went to his chamber to rest before supper, Abigail sighed. She knew her husband. There was no need to prepare the meal she had promised. She had learned long ago that when he was this drunk, he fell immediately into a deep slumber and could not be aroused until late in the morning. Just as well—she did not have the strength after all her adventures to prepare a large dinner.

She would tell him in the morning what she had done. He would be furious, not wanting to believe she had saved his life. He might even beat her. She shrugged. She had been beaten before.

The next morning, Abigail placed a small cup of wine beside Kenaz's bed. When he awoke, that would be the first thing he would reach for. Somehow those few sips of wine made him at least bearable until he fully recovered from his debauchery of the night before.

When he finally staggered out of the house into the sunlit courtyard, he covered his eyes with his hands. "Where are you, woman? I need you!"

Abigail sighed. It was always the same. "I'm here, my husband. I've baked fresh raisin cakes for your breakfast."

She hastily placed three cakes, still warm from the oven, on a plate and put it on the table. Kenaz sprawled on the bench. At first he pushed the plate away, but then he sniffed its fresh-baked aroma and began to nibble on one.

"Now, my lord husband." Abigail stood at the opposite side of the table facing him. "I would like to tell you where I was yesterday."

Kenaz grunted and reached for another raisin cake. Although he said nothing, he glared at her menacingly.

"When I learned that the outlaw David and his four hundred warriors were angered by your refusal of his request, I took a gift to him, hoping I could prevent him from killing us all."

"You what?"

Kenaz staggered to his feet, forgetting the unfinished raisin cake in his hand. His face began to turn purple above his beard.

"It's a good thing I did, my husband. David and his men were on their way here. He had sworn an oath before Yahweh that no male creature on your property would be alive by nightfall. I believe I saved your life."

Kenaz lurched forward and leaned on the table. He swept the plate with its remaining raisin cakes to the ground. Only the table between them prevented him from doing the same to her.

His breath came in gasps. "And what . . . did you . . . give him?"

Abigail took a step backward, changed her mind, and returned to the table. As long as the table was between them he could not strike her.

"My lord husband—" She tried to make her words firm but was more frightened of him than she had ever been of the outlaw David.

She bit her lip, then took a deep breath and continued. "I gave him two hundred loaves of bread—"

"Two hundred!"

". . . two barrels of wine—"

"Two barrels!"

". . . five dressed sheep, two bushels of roasted grain, two hundred fig cakes—"

"What?"

"I . . . and one hundred raisin cakes."

"One hundred—" Kenaz looked down at the raisin cake he still held in his hand. He blinked his eyes. The purple color in his face deepened. His mouth hung open.

Then with a curse, he flung the raisin cake to the ground and stamped on it. "You . . . you . . . I'll—"

Glaring at her, he took a step toward her, but the table was in his way. With a roar he lifted the heavy table and heaved it aside. His rage seemed to give him extra strength.

Abigail stepped backward, her hand going to her

throat. She had never seen him like this. He had been angry before, and sometimes on the morning after a drunken spree he had been mean-tempered. But never like this.

Suddenly he stopped. His face grew even darker. His eyes widened and his mouth gaped. His breath came in short rasping gasps.

And he fell heavily to the ground.

Abigail stared at him. He lay face down, unmoving, on the hard-packed courtyard earth. What had happened? After a few seconds of paralyzed fear, she went to him hesitantly. Kneeling, she turned him over. Kenaz seemed to be having trouble breathing.

He looked up at her, his eyes pleading. "Help . . . me!" he managed to gasp.

"Shua! Jarib! Come quickly!" she shouted.

When the two servants arrived, they helped her drag him to his bed chamber. He was heavy, his body bloated by years of overindulgence. It was hard to heave him onto the bed.

Abigail knelt beside him. He lay unmoving, his eyes closed. Was he dead? No. Occasionally he would grunt or wheeze and gasp for breath.

What should she do? She asked Shua to bring her a damp cloth, and she sponged off his face. What herbs could she brew into a tea for him? She didn't know, and even if she did, he might not be able to drink it. She had some medicinal oil in a flask which she had purchased from a caravan from the east. She might anoint his face with that to drive away the terrible color. But she suspected the problem was deeper than the color of his face. Something inside him.

Maybe God had touched him!

She caught her breath. Could it be true? Had God struck him down? If so, there was nothing she could do. But she had to do something. After all, she was his wife.

The rophe!

Zerahiah ben Uzzi, the Levite, lived in Carmel, only three miles away. He was a *rophe,* trained in the Israelite tradition of healers. Maybe he would know what to do. If he would lay hands on Kenaz, perhaps Yahweh would touch her husband and heal him.

"Jarib! Send for Zerahiah in Carmel."

Jarib had been standing near the door of the chamber, waiting for her orders. Now he seemed eager to do something.

"Yes, Mother Abigail. I'll send Hezro. With an extra donkey to bring the *rophe* here."

The old servant shuffled out. Abigail turned back to her husband. He was still alive, but unconscious. What more could she do? What could anybody do? Even the *rophe* could not heal—unless it was Yahweh's will.

Yahweh's will! Who could understand the mind of God? How could a mortal change Yahweh's mind? Could even a Levite persuade Yahweh to do something God didn't want to do? No. No humans, no matter how qualified by birth and training, could impose their will on the will of the Almighty.

Was this Yahweh's will? This illness, and possibly the death of her husband? Was Kenaz being punished for his sins? Was Yahweh that kind of a God? She shook her head. The questions were far beyond her ability to understand.

The *rophe* arrived—alone. When Abigail asked him where Hezro went, he shrugged.

"He went on an important mission. That was all he said."

Abigail frowned. What mission? Could he have gone to tell the outlaw David the news about Kenaz? But she quickly forgot that, as she hurried with the *rophe* into the bed chamber where Kenaz lay unconscious.

The Levite could do nothing for him. He anointed Kenaz with holy oil, but Abigail wondered how an oil blessed by a Levite *rophe* would be any better than the oil she had bought from the caravan. He prayed, chanting ancient psalms, but nothing helped.

Before sunset, the *rophe* rose to leave.

"I've done all I can," he muttered. "The rest is up to Yahweh."

Abigail nodded. That was probably a standard answer when the healer failed to heal. She gave the Levite several raisin cakes and a silver coin, then sent him back to Carmel.

The next day, Hezro returned. He came directly to Abigail.

"Where have you been?" she demanded, although she thought she knew the answer.

"To see David," he replied, his eyes meeting hers boldly. "I thought he should know."

"I see. And I suppose he ordered you to inform him immediately if Kenaz dies?"

"Yes, Mother Abigail."

The firmness in Abigail's voice deserted her.

"What will he do if my husband dies?"

Hezro regarded her solemnly.

"I don't know, my lady."

Nor do I, thought Abigail. But it led her to another thought, even more disturbing.

What will happen to me if Kenaz dies?

4

KENAZ WAS DYING. Abigail knew it as she knelt by his bedside day after day. There was little she could do: sponge off his face, try to feed him broth, make him comfortable as possible. During his conscious moments, he stared at her helplessly. He could not move.

On the fifth day, she sent a message to Kenaz's cousin, Jehallelel ben Naam of Bethlehem, that Kenaz was dying. There may have been other relatives, but she did not know them. Jehallelel would take care of that.

On the eighth day, Kenaz slipped into a coma from which he never awoke. Two days later, he died.

The mourning was loud, as custom demanded, but not enthusiastic. On the contrary, she sensed relief among all the servants in the household and in the field. Or was it that she was reading into their vocal grieving what she felt? But she must avoid such unfaithful thoughts. She had a responsibility to mourn her husband as a dutiful wife.

Jarib took charge of the funeral preparations, since he was the senior man in the household. He washed and anointed the body, dressed Kenaz in his best robe, and made sure the tomb was properly prepared. Only one more day could be spared before the corpse began to decay, and if any guests came to the funeral and smelled a rotting body, the dead man would be dishonored in the eyes of the family.

On the day of the burial, they could wait no longer. No relative had appeared to lead the procession to the tomb. Jarib, though only a servant, would have to do it.

Jarib chose six servants to carry the body. Hezro was not one of them; he had evidently gone to tell the outlaw David about Kenaz's death.

With loud wailing, the procession set out from the house. Jarib led the way, followed by the bier carried by six stout servants. Then came Abigail and all the others in the household.

Although Abigail's voice was hoarse from her keening and moaning, she nevertheless kept it up as loudly as she could. When Shua fell silent to rest her voice, Abigail glared at her until she at least made a token attempt to bewail the passing of her master. But the lamentation was subdued. Jarib quickened the pace. Though unconventional, this was thoughtful, since nobody was truly grieving and everyone wanted the process completed as soon as possible. The vocal part of the mourning ceased as soon as they reached the tomb.

Jarib and the six servants bearing the bier entered the cave, which had been prepared for Kenaz's burial many years before. Now the silence began.

Abigail was unprepared for the onslaught of silence. The contrast to the raucous wailing was so intense, she was startled to find new and disturbing thoughts assailing her. What would she do now? What about the kinsman Jehallelel, or any other relative who should be here to make decisions on Kenaz's affairs? Who would inherit? Who would supervise the estate?

And most disturbing of all: who would marry her?

Custom said the nearest relative should marry the widow. No, more than custom said this; the law of Moses required it. Jehallelel, Kenaz's cousin, was the mandated relative. She had seen him only once, at her wedding several years ago, and could remember nothing about him, not his age, the number of wives he already had, or anything about his personality.

Would it be possible for her to continue living here—without a husband? Be head of the household? Possible, yes. It had been done. But that could happen only if nobody wanted her. That was unlikely. She was young and desirable to any lusty man. More than that, she was rich. Marrying her would mean acquiring Kenaz's vast estate.

She stifled a sigh. Her future was not in her hands. Someone like Jehallelel or another relative would tell her—not ask her—what she must do.

"Abigail."

The voice spoke just behind her. A male voice. She frowned. Nobody should speak now. That was improper, disrespectful. Should she ignore it? Or turn and reprimand the speaker?

No. She could not. She would not. For she recognized that voice. Slowly she turned to face him.

The outlaw David had been incredibly quiet, to have sneaked up behind her without being noticed. Unless he had arrived during the time of wailing.

"Walk with me, my lady."

She couldn't do that. It was contrary to all convention. Indecent. But she only nodded and pushed her way through the mass of curious faces to go with him.

They walked in silence for a short distance.

Then David spoke, softly, "What will you do now?"

She almost didn't answer him. It was none of his business. But she answered anyway. "I'm not sure. Probably marry Kenaz's nearest kinsman."

"Who is. . . ?"

"Jehallelel ben Naam. I believe he's a cousin."

David frowned. His thumb and forefinger went to his chin in that familiar gesture. "Why isn't he here?"

"I don't know. We sent for him."

David regarded her solemnly for a moment. Then he nodded, as though he had just reached a decision. "No. You will not marry Jehallelel. He's old and fat, and has too many wives already. And he's mean. In a few years everybody would be calling him Nabal."

"Do you know him?"

David nodded. "He's from Bethlehem. That's where I grew up. Yes. I know him. And you must not marry him."

"But how can I—?"

"You will marry me."

Abigail gasped. She stared at him.

This was impossible. Ridiculous. David was an outlaw. A rebel against Yahweh's Anointed. She couldn't marry him. She couldn't. She wouldn't.

"Yes, my lord," she said quietly.

Why was she saying this? She had no right. It wasn't proper. It was . . . it was . . .

Unavoidable!

She couldn't say no. The decision was not hers. He had not asked her to marry him; he had told her. She could not refuse. She couldn't. Even if she wanted to. And . . . she didn't want to refuse.

That surprised her as much as the thought of marriage to rebel against Yahweh's Anointed.

"Tomorrow morning," he said softly.

Nothing more needed to be said. They rejoined the mourners at the tomb and stood in silence until Jarib and the others came out of the cave.

The return journey to the house was made in silence. As was proper. No word must be spoken until sundown. This was a time to sit in silence, to mourn the dead, to recall the past.

But Abigail's only thoughts were of the future.

5

ABIGAIL SLEPT poorly that night, although in the morning she wasn't sure if it was because she was fearful of the future or excited about it.

She arose early, roused the servants, and set them to preparing large quantities of food. For a wedding feast? No. To feed David's men. How many? She had heard that his entourage numbered about six hundred, but she couldn't be sure.

But Jarib knew. He had talked to Hezro and learned that about seventy men had come with him. Why? Was this his usual bodyguard? Or had they come to attend the funeral? Or . . . a wedding? Had David known before he had talked to her yesterday that he would marry her?

She sensed an excitement in the household which seemed out of place following the funeral of the master of the house. The servants went about their tasks laughing and shouting to one another. Abigail did not rebuke them. How could she? She felt the same.

Custom said she should not be seen by the bridegroom until the wedding. She should wear a veil. But she did neither. Custom would be ignored today. She was not a virginal bride for whom the wedding was the greatest day of her life. She had buried one husband yesterday and would marry another today. Customs had been shattered already.

The wedding feast did not seem a wedding feast. Although there was the sense of celebration and a goodly flow of wine, as was proper for any wedding, several glaring differences soon became apparent. David's men were the only guests, and they were not dressed for a festival. There was no father of the bride to make a speech, declare his daughter a virgin, and formally give her to the groom. No bridal chamber had been prepared. The festivities had about them a hurried air—just like the funeral—as though everyone wanted to get it over with and get on with more important things.

At noon David called his men together and they crowded into the courtyard. Not all of them, however—there wasn't room. Only about thirty fit. The others remained outside, surrounding the walls, spreading out into the estate, trampling on the garden. They seemed relaxed and in a celebrative mood, as young men at a wedding should be.

David's voice lifted above the buzz of conversation, calling for silence. They became quiet immediately. Something about him demanded full attention.

"Men of Judah." He spoke gravely, as though this were a formal oration. He might have been proclaiming a solemn assembly.

"I now take Abigail, widow of Kenaz, as my wife. Does anyone have any objections?"

The question was conventional, required in a formal announcement of marriage such as this. Of course, nobody spoke. There were no crude jokes. Only a somber, respectful silence.

A disturbance at the gate broke the mood of the wedding. A young man pushed his way through the crowd with some authority. Abigail recognized him from her last encounter with David's men. With an effort she recalled his name: Joab. One of David's lieutenants.

"What is it, Joab?" asked David.

"Visitors."

"Who?"

"Jehallelel, with about thirty armed men."

Abigail gasped. Would there be trouble? Would Kenaz's kinsman question David's bold action?

David frowned. His hand rose to stroke his chin. But when he spoke, his voice was calm. "All right. We'll wait for him."

A few minutes later, the crowd of young men parted to allow the newcomers to enter. A large palanquin carried by twelve sturdy youths led the procession, followed by the wealthy man's bodyguard. Many of David's men climbed the wall to make room for them. They found seats at the top of the wall to watch the proceedings.

With a practiced motion, the servants swung the huge chair to the ground. The curtains parted and Jehallelel stepped out.

Lurched out would be a better description. He was squat and fat, his beard gray and wiry, curling around his face. Cold cruel eyes peered out from under frowning brows. He glared at David, wheezing slightly.

"David ben Jesse." He spoke slowly, his words dripping with hatred. "I might have known. What's going on here?"

David's voice commanded attention.

"Jehallelel ben Naam. Welcome to a wedding feast."

Jehallelel looked around, his eyes darting to the armed men in the courtyard and on the walls. He had obviously seen the others outside. Then his eyes rested on Abigail.

"I came here for a funeral."

"That was yesterday." David spoke curtly. "Today we celebrate a wedding."

"Whose?" demanded Jehallelel, although he probably already knew.

"Mine. And the widow Abigail. Have you any objections?"

Abigail looked at Kenaz's cousin, who continued to glare at David. The question hung in the tense silence. A shrewd question. Perfectly timed. If Jehallelel failed to object, the wedding was valid.

Wedding custom demanded that the bride's relatives be given an opportunity to protest the match. Since there was no father to present his daughter, the nearest kinsman must validate the wedding. Had Jehallelel not shown up, the marriage could later be questioned. Now—if he did not object—it was legal.

"You already have a wife," he muttered.

David nodded. He spoke slowly. "Two, in fact."

Abigail compressed her lips. She had not known this.

"No," replied Jehallelel. "Just one. Saul, Yahweh's Anointed, has declared you dead and has given Michal to Palti ben Laish of Gallim."

David obviously had not heard this news. His face reddened; his jaw set. His hands closed into fists. Nevertheless, he held his fury inside him.

"Then she commits adultery, for she is still my wife." He paused, glaring at Jehallelel, then resumed speaking softly and deliberately. "So is Abigail—now. Do you object?"

The hush was ominous. Jehallelel's eyes darted around the assembled warriors. Some of David's men had already drawn their swords.

Jehallelel said nothing, but instead gave a brief shake of his head. The only response he could make—and live.

"Then," said David, his voice raising to a commanding level, "I declare in the presence of these guests and the family of Kenaz, that Abigail is now my legal wife. So let it be."

For several seconds more, Jehallelel glared at David.

Then he turned and crawled into his chair, closing the curtains abruptly. At a muffled order, the servants picked up the palanquin and marched out.

"You have made a powerful enemy, David," growled Joab.

David grinned recklessly. "Not for long. Only as long as he lives."

Joab laughed. And suddenly the solemn mood was broken by laughter from the men around them, as their natural good humor returned.

The only person not laughing, it seemed, was Abigail.

Her excited feeling had gone, driven away by David's last words. She knew what he meant.

And, she wondered, was that a glimpse into the life ahead of her? What kind of a man did she marry?

6

DAVID WAS a gentle and considerate lover. Abigail was amazed and delighted, following the experiences with a brutal and often drunken Nabal. She felt a twinge of guilt at comparing the old husband with the new in their ability to please a marriage partner. She looked forward to many more nights of love and passion.

In the morning she arose early to bake raisin cakes, feeling sure her present husband would appreciate them more than her former. There—she had done it again. That subtle comparison between David and Nabal. She must not do that. Ever. It wasn't fair to Nabal.

Nabal! Why couldn't she say Kenaz? Even in the privacy of her thoughts, she called him what everybody else did: the Fool. She shook her head in wonderment. How quickly everything had changed in her life! And how drastically! With David, everything would be different.

Where would he take her? To the wilderness, to share the dangerous—and exciting!—life of an outlaw? There she would have to face the fact that she could lose her new husband at any time—each time he went out on his raids, or faced the trained warriors of King Saul.

King Saul, Anointed One of Yahweh! And David, renegade, rebel, outcast of Israel—her husband! What would become of her? Would she end up facing a grisly death when the royal Israelite army defeated the rebels and destroyed their camp? Or . . . would she some day become queen of Israel? And mother of the next Anointed One?

No, she couldn't become queen of Israel. She was the third wife. Even if the first wife, Michal, had been discredited by marrying—or committing adultery with—another man, she was still of royal blood and the first wife.

Then there was that other wife, the one who lived in David's wilderness camp. Abigail would soon be sharing wifely duties with her. What would she be like? Would there be jealousy? Would this wife lord it over Abigail?

She shook her head as she thought about all these changes coming so suddenly. The future was so uncertain! She didn't know whether to dread it or embrace it!

"Yahweh's blessings on you, wife!"

David's voice! She spun around, dropping a raisin cake on the courtyard ground. He stood in the doorway, hair and beard immaculately groomed, smiling, fully dressed, "like a bridegroom emerging from his chamber," as the ancient psalm said.

She caught her breath. He looked . . . magnificent! He was shining as brightly as the sun, emerging from the colorful sunrise in the east, ready to run its course through the heavens! She smiled, feeling a surge of energy and love swelling in her body. She faced a new day with this brilliant sun, and she would run the course with him!

He strode forward briskly, energetically, and took her in his arms. The kiss on her lips was tender. The day—and week—ahead would be glorious.

"Thank you for a wonderful night," he murmured, his lips barely moving against her cheek. "I only regret that I can't stay to enjoy a few more."

She luxuriated in the security of the arms which held her. Such strong arms. She felt so safe.

And then the meaning of his last statement struck her. "What . . . what do you mean?"

He looked into her eyes. He seemed genuinely sad.

"I regret I must leave. My business today is urgent."

"But. . . ."

She wasn't able to say what she wanted to say. That the wedding night was only a beginning, not an end. That custom demanded a whole week of bliss following a marriage. That . . . the sun was setting back into the east, even before its light had fully banished the darkness.

"I'm sorry. Truly sorry. I wish I could stay." He gazed at her with the same compassion she had experienced last night. The same tenderness. The same love.

"But I'll send for you soon. And we will have many more happy nights ahead of us."

She wanted to ask why. Why couldn't he stay? Where was he going? Why didn't he take her with him? What would become of her? Why did he . . . ? She should speak—now—but her voice froze. She couldn't talk.

"Goodbye, my love," he whispered, and kissed her firmly on the mouth. Then he released her, grabbed a handful of raisin cakes, and strode out of the courtyard.

She stood there, dazed, uncomprehending. She hadn't yet fully realized what had happened. He had left her. Just like that. With such an abrupt goodbye.

Her knees buckled; she sank to the ground. Before her lay the raisin cake she had dropped moments before. The raisin cake meant for David. Now dirty. Forgotten. Alone.

She didn't know how long she sat there. The sounds of excited activity outside the courtyard made no impression on her. Soon they too faded away. But all she saw was the forlorn raisin cake on the ground before her.

Shua found her there, tenderly raised her, and led her to her bed. There she slept. Slept soundly. Losing herself in the depth of slumber, a welcome refuge from the realities of life. And disillusionment.

7

THE DAYS stumbled by, one as dreary as the next. David had left behind a bodyguard consisting of thirty men. Their leader was Hezro's kinsman Shammah ben Agee. Abigail remembered him as the crude outlaw who had made an insulting remark to her when she first met David. His wife, Miriam, now shared the house with Abigail and Shua.

There was little for the bodyguard to do. They spread themselves out over the estate, tending sheep, working the gardens, or just lounging in the courtyard talking idly.

Shua fed them. Abigail avoided them.

She could not avoid Shammah, however. He seemed to force his company upon her. At first she resented him, with his boorish manners and brash talk. But as the days turned into weeks, he became a diversion. At least it was something to do while waiting for David to send for her.

"Mother Abigail." Shammah at least used the respectful title while addressing her, undoubtedly out of respect for David. "Let me tell you about the time I killed eighty Philistines in what is now known as 'The Battle of the Lentil Field.' All my men had fled the field—"

He launched into a tale of heroism about his exploits as a warrior. Hezro, who had come to the house to visit Shua, to whom he was betrothed, rolled his eyes and grinned.

Shammah became for Abigail a savior from the lonely,

depressing days. He told his preposterous stories with a flair, held Abigail's attention, and even elicited some hearty laughs.

He was also a valuable source of information. Through him, Abigail learned of David's activities and adventures.

"David, not Saul, is Yahweh's true Anointed," he told her one day.

She didn't know whether to believe him. She had heard that the outlaw claimed to be the rightful king of Israel, but like most sensible people in Israel, she had rejected this as common gossip. Perhaps a deliberate lie spread around by David himself, to gain support for his cause.

"It's true," insisted Shammah. "Yahweh's prophet Samuel himself anointed him."

Shammah continued with one of his grand stories. The prophet Samuel, he said, visited Jesse's home near Bethlehem, looking closely at Jesse's six stalwart sons. He rejected all of them. He then learned of the youngest who tended the sheep. Samuel had anointed David in the pasture in the presence of his family.

And Shammah told of David's visit to the camp of King Saul, when the Israelite army had gone out to meet the Philistines in battle. "Goliath, a Philistine giant, challenged any son of Israel to meet him in individual combat. Nobody dared—until David came along."

The story Shammah told in such minute detail—he had been there, he claimed—described how the youngster David, with no armor, nothing more than his shepherd's slingshot, went out to face the giant.

"One stone! That's all it took. One stone! And the giant fell to the ground with a thud that shook the earth!"

Again Abigail didn't know whether to believe him. She had heard the story before. The Israelite hero was not a shepherd boy with a slingshot, but a skilled warrior named Elhanon Ben Jairs. She said as much to Shammah.

"You're wrong, Mother Abigail. Elhanon defeated in single combat Goliath's brother Lahmi. You may ask Elhanon when you next see him. He is one of David's Mighty Three—as I am."

"You're confused, Cousin." Hezro, ordinarily quiet while Shammah told his tales, now interrupted. "Elhanon is one of the Mighty *Thirty*. Eliazer ben Dodo is one of the Mighty *Three*, along with you and Adino the Ezrite. And you're there only because you talked yourself in."

This brought a loud and sputtering rebuttal from Shammah, as Hezro lapsed into his usual silence.

As the days passed, Abigail became aware of the dwindling numbers of sheep and goats. One evening she asked Shammah about it.

"Yes, Mother Abigail. They're going to Ziklag."

"Ziklag!"

The city of the Sea Peoples—whom Shammah called the Philistines—lay far to the southwest, at the edge of the desert.

Shammah grinned. "It's David's city now. The Philistine king Achish gave it to him. Ran everybody out of the city, and they weren't too happy about it. But it was a smart move on King Achish's part. Now he has David as his buffer state between him and the Egyptians."

"Are you saying," asked Abigail, "Achish is using David to guard his back while he makes war on Israel?"

Shammah's grin faded into a frown. Perhaps he had not expected such a shrewd political insight from a woman.

"I suppose so. But it's to David's advantage too. He now has a safe place to live—and bring his family."

"Then I assume," said Abigail, "that's where we're going when David sends for us?"

"Right, Mother Abigail. That's why he's sending your late husband's wealth to Ziklag now. This should be enough to keep us all fat and happy for a long time. And especially when you think of those Amalekite cities to the south which we can raid now and then."

Ziklag. Her future home. A city already established. Where she will be living . . . along with that other wife.

"Tell me, Shammah. David's other wives. What are they like?"

Shammah leaned back against the wall and took a sip of wine.

"Michal." He spoke slowly, frowning. "She's Saul's daughter. Uppity. Demanding. Shrewish. She certainly has an acid tongue! David couldn't stand her. When Saul married her off to someone else, he should have let her go. But David considers that a direct insult to Yahweh's Anointed. Some day, he'll get her back. Huh! Then he'll wish he hadn't."

So will I, probably, mused Abigail. Aloud she said, "So David never truly loved her?"

"He did, at first. They were both young then. Do you know what bride price King Saul demanded from him to marry his daughter?"

Abigail shook her head. David's father was rich, so it must be some fabulous amount.

Shammah grinned. "Two hundred foreskins!"

Abigail gasped. That meant he had to kill two hundred people.

"Philistines?" she asked.

Shammah nodded. "And him just a kid who still had sheep dung on his sandals."

Miriam, Shammah's wife, dug her elbow into his side. "Watch your words, donkey. Remember who you're talking to," she said.

Shammah rolled his eyes, although the grin did not disappear from his face. Not many men in Israel would accept that kind of teasing from his wife.

Shammah continued. "In those days, King Saul hated David. Some say he was jealous, because everybody liked that shepherd kid better than the king himself. The warriors sang songs about David."

Abigail had heard rumors about that—a marching song, something about "Saul has slain his thousands and David his ten thousands." She could see how a proud man would be jealous.

Shammah took another gulp of wine.

"Most people were saying a kind of madness afflicted the king. Yahweh had touched him. That's what I think. Saul had the melancholies. He brooded—all the time. He could change suddenly, and become energetic and strong, then lapse back into depression. Only David's harp playing and singing seemed to please him."

"Wasn't David afraid of him?"

"Yes, and with good reason. Once Saul threw his spear at David. No warning. Just heaved it."

"Was that why David became an outlaw? Because Saul drove him out?"

"Yes." Shammah nodded his head vigorously. "Jonathan helped him get away. Jonathan was David's best friend in those days."

Jonathan—King Saul's son. Heir to the throne. Of all people who should be David's enemy, it should be Jonathan.

"Michal, too," continued Shammah. "She helped him escape."

Michal. She must have loved David very much. But no more, evidently. Too much had happened. She now had another husband. Was she bitter? Or did she still love the dashing youth who had rebelled against her father?

"Now Shammah, tell me about David's other wife. What's she like?"

"Ahinoam. A pretty girl. A widow from Jezreel."

"Jezreel?" Abigail frowned. "That isn't far from here."

"That's right. The Jezreel near Hebron, not the plain up north. Her husband was a large landowner until he died. By marrying her, David could keep us fed for a year—"

He broke off, his face coloring. Abigail nodded. She understood his embarrassment. The implication stared at her boldly. That was how David chose his wives: those who were wealthy and could support him.

Soon she would move to Ziklag, where her wealth would sustain David for another year. And live with Ahinoam, who supported David last year.

She sighed. How many more wives would David marry—so he could carry on his war of rebellion?

Eventually, the messengers from David arrived telling Abigail to be prepared to leave for Ziklag the next day. This came as no surprise to her, as the last of her flocks had departed for her new home. Only a small bodyguard remained, along with Jarib and Shua and four wives of men in the bodyguard.

The messengers also told her to wait for the arrival of Ahinoam, David's second wife. They would travel together to Ziklag.

What would she be like? Would she be domineering? Aloof? Embittered by David's squandering her wealth? Or —worst of all—would she be so beautiful she commanded first place in David's affections?

When Ahinoam arrived on a donkey, she greeted Abigail cordially, much to Abigail's relief. She had at least thirty men in her bodyguard. A train of servants and ox-drawn wagons carrying many possessions followed.

Abigail's greeting was equally cordial, although she spoke formally and somewhat fearfully to the woman with whom she would share her life—and husband.

"Welcome to Carmel, my lady. The day is almost gone. Come inside and rest. Tomorrow we journey to Ziklag."

Ahinoam smiled shyly. "Good idea. That will give us a chance to become better acquainted."

How could she possibly dislike this girl? Abigail bit her lip as she turned away. Was she disappointed? Had she expected to find her so obnoxious that hating her would be easy? If Ahinoam turned out to be a pleasant companion, would Abigail be able to accept her? Even become friends?

As she directed the servants to prepare a feast worthy of her guest, she studied David's other wife surreptitiously. Ahinoam's slender body and smooth-skinned face made her appear about the same age as Abigail—in her late teens. Dark complexion. Raven hair, black eyebrows. Dark eyes. Narrow face. Large nose. Thin lips. Pointed chin. In spite of Shammah's description of her—"very pretty!"—she was not exceptionally beautiful—until she smiled. Then her dark face suddenly became radiant, softening her personality and transforming her into someone who was at the same time humble, sensitive, unspoiled.

Abigail didn't know whether to be attracted to her—or repelled. Ahinoam showed none of the qualities Abigail expected—haughtiness, condescension, arrogance. She should be like that; after all, she was the second wife and Abigail the third. But she wasn't.

She was attractive. And if attractive to Abigail, she would be attractive to David.

Their conversation was superficial, as though by making small talk they could avoid asking the questions which hung unanswered in the air between them. How was David as a lover? How would they share their time with him when he was home? Would they be forced to live in the same house? Who would manage the household? Who would David like best?

But this kind of discussion would come later, as familiarity made them either talkative friends or silent enemies.

8

ZIKLAG, ACCORDING to Shammah, was a typical Philistine city. Following the conquest, the city had been assigned by Joshua to the tribe of Simeon. It had been built by the Simeonites as an Israelite city at the edge of the mountains at the beginning of the broad coastal plain, just northeast of Beersheba. Then the Sea Peoples —the Philistines, they called themselves—invaded and settled along the coast. They had conquered Ziklag and it became their southern outpost city.

The city of Ziklag impressed Abigail. The Israelites who conquered it had rebuilt it as a stronghold. It boasted thick walls and a massive gate. Impregnable. It could never be conquered; she would be safe here.

Two large houses, located on the large square by the central well, had been reserved for David's wives. Abigail's new home was typically Canaanite: a walled courtyard with a two-story building at one side. The cleanliness impressed her, until she learned that the former Philistine owners, disgruntled by their sudden displacement at the order of King Achish, had left it a mess, with broken pottery shards, dead animals, and human excrement defacing every inch of property. She never did learn who cleaned it up for her.

She had barely settled into the home, with her servants Jarib and Shua, when David arrived in Ziklag after one of his raids. First he went to Ahinoam's house next door, much to Abigail's dismay. But he stayed only a few minutes before crossing the square to enter the courtyard where Abigail stood to welcome her husband home.

He came eagerly to her, took her in his arms, and kissed her tenderly.

"Abigail, my love," he murmured in her ear. "I hope you are comfortable here."

"Yes, my husband."

She tried to master her voice, although it trembled slightly. With his strong arms around her, she understood how David could command love from everyone around him, even when his actions sometimes left them with emotion which from anyone else would have turned into hatred and resentment.

"I'll be here a week before I have to leave again. And I'll spend it here. This will be the bridal week we had to miss when we were married."

Another wave of joy swept through Abigail. A week! The promised bridal week, which allowed husband and wife to become intimately acquainted, assuring them of a long and happy relationship together. Marriage—the wise Creator's way of combining the mundane function of procreation with the exquisite bliss of erotic love—this was the fulfillment of dreams. She felt like a virginal bride, experiencing the ecstasy of her first marriage week.

But as always these days when a happy thought captured her consciousness, a guilty thought pushed its way into her mind, destroying her serenity. Was she ecstatic about David's coming to her first? Or was this just the exultation of victory over her rival next door? The thought was unworthy; she struggled to banish it.

The week was indeed blissful. David was a gentle and sensitive lover. The moments of rapture she experienced in his bed were like nothing she had known. His conversation with her during the days was lively and imaginative. Since they were out of view of other people, he treated her as an equal. Her mind, so long idle because of a lack of an equal companion, eagerly met the stimulating challenge and plunged into new unexplored areas. He listened to her, took her seriously, and plumbed her mind as he would with one of his lieutenants. She felt honored.

And laughter! Her husband had a creative wit. She often found herself rocking with laughter at his stories. She too invented some wild tales, which brought gales of laughter from an appreciative husband.

He sang for her, and she marveled at the beauty of his voice. Something about it was different. Not just the clear tenor quality, the lilting cadence of his psalms and ballads, but something more, something profound. As he sang, she felt she could see into the depth of his being. And she saw there a sensitive soul, thoughtful, imaginative, and genuinely religious.

On the last day of the bridal week, he sang a psalm he had composed during his youth. "Yahweh is *my* shepherd. I have everything I want. He leads me to a place of rest in the meadow grass. He brings me to a quiet pool of water, where I can lie down to restore my soul. He shows me the right paths for my life, because his name is Yahweh."

Abigail listened, her eyes closed, picturing a small boy in the wilderness leading his sheep. The boy was alone. Then Yahweh came to him and walked beside him. And the boy was alone no longer. The song continued.

"Even when I walk down that dark valley called 'The Shadow of Death,' I have no fear. You are always with me, Yahweh. Your rod and staff are my comfort. You provide food for me each day, in the very presence of my enemies. My cup overflows! I know that throughout my life, your goodness and love will follow me. At the end, I will go to live in your house forever."

Abigail sat in silence for a long moment after the song ended. Finally she opened her eyes and looked at him. "It's beautiful, David."

He smiled. "It's not finished. I don't suppose it will ever be finished. Each time I sing it, I refine it a little more."

"I don't see how you can improve it."

"It's like . . . well, like the time I spend with Yahweh. Every day he comes to me, and every day my song changes. I don't think my psalm will ever be finished."

But the week was finished. The time had passed, faster than any week in her life.

"Today," he told her, "I must leave. I'm sorry. I wish I didn't have to. I would love to stay here with you forever."

He held her in his arms and kissed her. That familiar dizzying wave swept through her. Some day he would return. When he did, this rapture could continue.

As before, when a blissful thought filled her mind, another thought pushed its way in, destroying her peace, plaguing her with guilt. Did he have a week such as this with Ahinoam? And before that, with Michal? Was it as pure, as supremely happy, as profoundly intimate, as this one? Did he sing the plaintive shepherd's song for them? Did he love Ahinoam as much as he loved her?

Very soon after he had gone, she sat alone in her courtyard. Jarib and Shua, respecting her silence, avoided her. But not Ahinoam. David's other wife appeared at the gate and burst in on her.

At first Abigail's resentment left her sullen and unresponsive to Ahinoam's expressions of concern.

"I felt the same way when he left," she told Abigail, her voice soft and genuinely sympathetic. "For days, I cried. And I was alone. I had no one to comfort me."

"Thank you, Ahinoam. I'm quite all right. But I do appreciate your concern. You should be jealous. Instead, you are kind. Thank you."

55

Ahinoam smiled. "If it will make you feel any better, I will tell you why he spent no time with me. I am with child. David no longer needs me. If I bear him a son, he will be pleased, but until you too are pregnant, he will spend all his free time in your house, not mine."

"Oh!"

Abigail stared at Ahinoam. Again the dual thoughts pushed their way into her mind. She was genuinely happy for Ahinoam. A wife's greatest gift to her husband was a son, an heir. Nothing would please a loving marital companion more than to give him the one thing no amount of wealth or power could purchase.

The other thought was not as kind. Ahinoam had conceived first. Her son would be the heir. But more than just an heir. He would be the prince of Israel. The lawful ascendant to the throne. The Anointed One of Yahweh.

And Abigail, if she ever conceived and bore a son for her husband, would have nothing. Her son would be just another servant of the king.

An even more disturbing thought pushed itself into her mind. Was that why David had spent a blissful week with her and avoided Ahinoam's tent? Was that why he was so loving and solicitous toward her? Because he already had what he wanted most—from Ahinoam?

Abigail burst into tears, much to the dismay of Ahinoam. What she had mistaken for love from her husband was not love. It was something entirely different.

David's only reason for marrying her was to gain her property. The blissful week they had just spent together was to obtain from her a backup heir to the throne. He was using his wives, using them without loving them, using them just for his own selfish ends.

Only one thing mattered to her husband—his ambition. He cared nothing for anybody, his men, his wives. Only the throne. Only the throne.

She sobbed and would not be comforted.

As time passed, Abigail came to accept David's ambition—even respect it. He was only acting as a king should. He must establish a dynasty. To do that required sons. And to have sons required wives, several wives. His household must grow, and she would not be the last of the wives.

She could not thwart her husband's plans for the future, even if she wanted to. And she didn't want to. On the contrary, she found herself wanting to do all she could to further his regal aspirations.

Part of her acceptance of David's ambition, she came to admit, was due to his charm. He was a sensitive lover. He came to her bed every night he spent in Ziklag—hers, not Ahinoam's, for obvious reasons. Those nights of passion were so blissful that Abigail looked forward to them and built her life around them. She came to regard her life at Ziklag as a paradise comparable to the Eden in the Sacred Story.

One night David said to her, "You are my first wife."

Abigail said nothing. She stared at him, the question undoubtedly written on her face. An obvious question.

David laughed, and answered it. "I know you were not the first one I married. Michal was. She should be the first wife. But she forfeited that right when Saul gave her to someone else. She is still my wife, because no one can usurp the wife of Yahweh's Anointed. But she shall not be the mother of my sons, nor shall she be the first wife."

Abigail nodded. David used the term "first wife" to mean the leader of his household, not the first in order of marriage.

In a household where there were several wives, one held authority. Long tradition established that to be the first woman he married—not the one her husband designated.

It wasn't the law of Moses which governed this, only custom. Mosaic Law in fact never sanctioned polygamy, recognizing it only as a reality which could not be avoided. But it never mentioned who had the right of leadership in a household of multiple wives.

Only once did the law of Moses say anything at all about the rights of wives, and that had more to do with their children. Abigail once heard a priest declare, "If a man has two wives, one loved and the other unloved, and both have sons, the firstborn shall be the heir, *even though he is the son of the unloved one.*" This meant Ahinoam's son would be the heir to the throne, even if Abigail was David's favorite.

Abigail wondered how Ahinoam would feel about this. The thought prompted her next question. "Why *me?*" she asked. "Why not Ahinoam, who will be mother of your firstborn?"

David smiled and held her tightly. "Ahinoam is—well . . . Ahinoam. She can't handle it. You, my dear, deserve the honor of first wife. You alone. Because I love you."

"And I love you," she murmured in reply.

She understood what he really meant, and it had nothing to do with his declared love for her. He was being kingly again.

The first wife, in David's thinking, would rule the king's household. She would control the other wives and children. All the petty jealousies, the jockeying for power, each one maneuvering to have her own son ascend the throne—only a strong hand could manage a king's household. Perhaps Michal could have done it, but David would not allow it. Ahinoam was meek, unable to assert her will on others.

Could Abigail? From David's viewpoint she could. He had seen how she had handled her former husband's acts of foolishness. He knew of the respect and obedience given her by the servants. He would see her as the obvious choice for first wife.

And so she accepted the responsibility. Accepted it because she loved her husband. He was being regal, his ambition asserting itself. And she would help him. Just because he asked her.

But the thought occurred to her again—how would Ahinoam accept this?

Her relationship to Ahinoam during the days which followed grew into a deep friendship partly, she had to admit to herself, because the other wife was no threat to her. As long as Ahinoam was pregnant, David did little more than drop in at her house for a brief visit before coming to Abigail's house to spend the night. She marveled that Ahinoam showed no resentment toward Abigail for those nights.

Ahinoam's slim waist swelled and quivered with life, much to the future mother's delight. Abigail's, too. They spent many happy hours together, feeling and listening to the tiny life beating and jumping inside the womb. Boy or girl? Ahinoam felt sure it was a boy, and Abigail could not disagree. If the father were indeed a favorite of Yahweh, then this was a part of God's plan for Israel.

The first-born son of Yahweh's Anointed! The line of succession would be assured—through Ahinoam, not Abigail. Abigail felt no resentment, no jealousy. She would gladly trade being the mother of the heir to the throne for those blissful nights of love with her husband.

And besides, she told herself, she did not want to be the mother of a future king. That could hold only grief in the years ahead.

But what would the years ahead hold for her as the first wife in a king's household?

9

BEFORE AHINOAM'S baby was born, Abigail herself conceived.

David's boyish enthusiasm reflected his regal ambitions. "Now I shall have two sons!" he exclaimed. " Two boys, to assure my dynasty!"

"What if it's a girl?" Abigail could hardly contain her amusement. "That does happen, you know."

"Not to Yahweh's Anointed! Not until my dynasty has been firmly established. Then I will have a few daughters, to give in marriage to neighboring kings."

Abigail laughed, sharing his happiness. But she knew that in David's mind, wives and children were all dedicated to one goal: insuring his kingdom.

Ahinoam's time drew near; she gave birth to a boy. She named him Amnon.

"I talked it over with David," she confided in Abigail one day. "We decided on Amnon together."

Abigail smiled. Knowing both Ahinoam and David, she could guess how the conversation went. David, with his usual charm, could lead his wife into thinking it was a joint decision, when most likely David knew in advance what the child's name would be.

"And why did you choose Amnon?" she asked. The name meant "faithful."

"Because we want this child always to be reminded to

be faithful to Yahweh, since he will be the Anointed One some day. You know what happened to King Saul when he turned aside from Yahweh. God deserted him."

Abigail nodded. That sounded like David. Perhaps he even had another meaning hidden in the name: he wanted the boy to remember always to be loyal to his father, and never do anything to embarrass or diminish the rightful king of Israel.

As Abigail's body swelled with new life, David came to her less often. His raids on the Amalekites to the south occupied his attention. Nevertheless, when he did visit her he charmed her with wit, good humor, and tenderness. She enjoyed his visits most when he discussed with her what Ahinoam called "the business of men." And when Abigail offered an opinion, David listened intently.

"We raided the Girzites yesterday," he told her once. "They are a primitive people, not related to the Amalekites. Not much plunder, but they had a sturdy breed of goats which we added to our herd."

Abigail asked him solemnly, "Were you in danger?"

"No. They are a small tribe, poorly trained to fight against our warriors." David smiled indulgently. "But you must never worry about me, my love."

"But I do. I wouldn't want anything to happen to the father of my child."

"Nothing will. Remember, I am Yahweh's Anointed. God has plans for my future." He patted her swollen belly gently. "And for our son."

"And what did you tell King Achish today?"

For several months, while they had lived in the Philistine city of Ziklag under King Achish's protection, David had given the impression of fighting against Israelites rather than Canaanites. King Achish believed David had cut all ties with Israel, and now lived as an independent king under the vassalage of the Philistines.

David chuckled. "I told him we attacked the people of Jerahmeel. He believed it."

The people of Jerahmeel were Kenites who had been a part of the Israelite migration from Egypt. Many people thought of them as Israelites, including King Achish.

"David, what if King Achish learns the truth about your raids? He could, you know. He isn't stupid."

"Not much chance." David stroked his chin with his thumb and forefinger. "There's nobody alive to tell him."

Abigail shuddered. How hard it was for her to accept the fact that her mild-mannered, boyish husband was a hardened killer, who wouldn't hesitate to order the total assassination of all the people in a city he had just conquered. Women. Children. Babies. But she knew it happened. Everybody knew—except King Achish.

Abigail's time drew near for delivery. On a cold rainy day she gave birth to a beautiful child. A boy, much to David's delight.

"Praise Yahweh!" exclaimed David, when he first held his son in his arms. "God has judged me, and I am vindicated!"

Abigail stared at her husband. What did he mean by that? Was it just the pious statement of a man who deeply believed in the reality of his God, or was there something hidden behind his words?

She was about to ask him, when suddenly he placed the child on her knees. The custom of naming a child on his mother's knees went back a long way in Israel's history. This was a significant moment.

They had not discussed the naming of the child. Abigail, when she first looked at the baby, decided to propose "Chileab," meaning "resembling his father." The child was fair, lighter in complexion than many Israelites. Lighter than Amnon, who bore the dark face and skin of his mother Ahinoam.

There was another reason, however, for naming the child Chileab. About a year had passed since she had been married to David. David's enemies—and there would be many in the future—would be happy to point out that this child could well be the son of Kenaz of Carmel, Abigail's former husband. But the name Chileab would say to them, *Just look at him. You know whose son he is.*

And now the child rested on her knees, held by David's strong hands. The time had come for naming him. According to ancient custom, the mother had the right to select the name.

"His name is Chileab," said Abigail softly.

"No, my love."

David's smile faded from his face. He looked at her coldly. Abigail, absorbing that gaze, knew why he could order the slaughter of women, children, even babies. She knew also that the naming of the baby would not be her prerogative.

"His name is Daniel." David's voice had the strength of iron.

Abigail nodded. "His name is Daniel," she echoed.

The name meant, "God has judged." Abigail recalled the cryptic words David had spoken when he held the boy in his arms. *God has judged me, and I am vindicated.* She thought she understood.

Ever since their marriage, David had dropped hints of his uneasiness over marrying the wife of a man he had sworn to kill. He had said loudly and volubly that God, not David, had killed Nabal. Nobody disputed that, but there were rumors. The rumors had disturbed David more than most of the wild rumors which always accompanied a famous person. Perhaps because he himself felt responsible for Nabal's death, his uneasiness was reflected in the name he gave the son of Nabal's widow.

David's guilt was unjustified, Abigail knew. Kenaz had

died of natural causes; in fact, his own gluttony and fierce temper had led to his death. But a person's guilt can be real and unsettling, whether justified or not. And by naming his child Daniel, he could ease the burden of guilt he carried.

One evening, when David came to visit her, he wore a worried frown. "I think Achish distrusts me," he told her.

Abigail nodded. This news did not surprise her. She had long suspected that the Philistine king would learn that David was not at war with Israel but only raided the tribes to the south.

"What will he do?" she asked.

David shrugged. "Nothing, I suppose. We're too powerful an ally for him to attack us. But . . . there are other things."

"What, my husband?"

David pinched his chin with his thumb and forefinger. "He's planning a campaign against Saul soon, after the sheep shearing. He wants our men to join his army."

Abigail regarded her husband thoughtfully.

"And that will mean going into battle against Yahweh's Anointed," she murmured.

David nodded, his face solemn. "And there's no way I can refuse."

Abigail reached out and touched his hand. "What will you do?"

David grinned, and something of his boyish recklessness showed in his face. "We'll go with him, of course." His words came out light and carefree. "And trust in Yahweh to take care of us."

"And if he doesn't?"

David turned and looked down on the baby, sleeping peacefully in his cradle. "He will."

Gently he rocked the tiny bed. "He always has in the past. Why shouldn't he now?"

In the days that followed, the city of Ziklag feverishly prepared for the departure. The sheep were sheared early, and the women of the city looked forward to the pleasant task of spinning the wool into yarn and weaving garments for their men when they returned from war. It would at least keep them busy in the lonely days ahead.

To her dismay, Abigail learned that nearly all the men in David's army were going with King Achish. Only a small squad of thirty men would be left behind to guard the city. No matter—the city's walls were sturdy, and they had nothing to fear from the nearby tribes, whom David had decimated in his raids during the past year.

Nevertheless, Abigail felt a strange foreboding as the men marched out of the city. Six hundred warriors, well-trained, battle-hardened—a powerful force against any enemy. And behind them? A city of women and children, naked and vulnerable, with only thirty warriors to protect them.

And a wall. Sturdy gates. David's reputation, which would lead to swift and ruthless retaliation if anyone attacked.

And of course Yahweh.

Abigail sighed. If only she had as much faith as her husband in God's protective arm.

10

ABIGAIL AWOKE with a start. Someone had screamed. Or was it a shout? She heard it again, from outside the house, somewhere in the city. A man's shout. And a woman's scream.

She leaped out of bed and dressed hurriedly. What had happened? Had the men returned already? But it was only two weeks since they left.

A cold hand gripped her heart as realization dawned on her. The city was under attack. Or worse—conquered. The enemy, whoever it was, was already in the gates.

She picked up her sleeping baby and stepped into the courtyard. The dawn's dusky light showed the gate of their house closed and barred, but that wouldn't deter a determined enemy. The house was not built for defense; the bar was weak. What should she do?

Jarib stepped out of the house, spear in hand.

"Please, Jarib. Put the spear down. You can't stand up against them. You'll only be killed."

"No, Mother Abigail. I'll—"

Voices came to them from just outside the gates. Excited voices, spouting undecipherable gibberish. Jarib stepped in front of Abigail, spear held in front.

A crash sounded at the gate, then another. The sturdy doors buckled; the flimsy bar splintered. The gates flew open and about ten men poured through from the street.

They were short men, heavily bearded, wearing animal skins and leggings. Their weapons were swords and slingshots.

Jarib bravely faced them, but his courage was not enough. A stone from a slingshot brought him down, and a sword pierced his throat. Abigail watched in horror as her devoted servant's life poured out on the ground in front of her.

The men circled her, grinning. One seemed the leader. He spoke commands in a strange language, and several of the warriors entered the house. They came out almost immediately, dragging Shua with them. Abigail was glad to see she was dressed.

The leader gave more orders. Four of the men grasped Abigail and Shua by the arms and pulled them out the broken gate. Abigail glanced behind and glimpsed the men entering the house, probably to loot it.

In the street, she discovered she was not the only prisoner. Their captors herded a large group of women and small children down the street toward the city gate. Their screams and moans subsided somewhat at the sight of Abigail.

Where was Ahinoam? And her son Amnon, David's heir? Yes, there they were, among the other women and children. They seemed unharmed.

But there were no men. Evidently the orders had been to kill all men in the city and take prisoner all women and small children. As they were shoved or dragged out through the city gate, Abigail surveyed the prisoners. There were several hundred women altogether, wives or servants of David's men.

They looked to her for leadership. Abigail clutched baby Daniel to her and held her head high.

"Courage, friends," she said, calmly as she could. "We must show them what Israelite women are made of."

The words seemed to quiet them. Even the children ceased their whimpering.

Their guards halted them about a hundred paces from the city. Abigail watched as more and more warriors poured out through the city gates, loaded with plunder. Some of them had taken the time to hitch up oxen to carts laden with treasures from the houses. David's men had accumulated considerable wealth on their many raids to the south. Soon a wisp of smoke began to rise from the conquered city.

As flames shot into the sky behind them, the procession began, heading south. Abigail estimated about five hundred men, although she could not see them all to get an accurate count. Behind them trailed the ox-drawn carts filled with their new riches, and behind that a cloud of dust arose from the flocks and herds.

Who were these raiders? Amalekites, probably. David had often spoken of his enemies, describing them as savages who dressed in skins. Although he had raided and decimated their villages, there were so many of them that the survivors had evidently forged an alliance to attack Ziklag and deal a blow to the Israelite who had tormented them so long.

Unfortunately, they had come just two weeks after David's men had left the city naked and vulnerable. This thought brought a frown to Abigail's forehead. Had they been told when to attack? If so, who had betrayed them? Could it have been King Achish? His suspicions about David's allegiance might have turned him from ally into treacherous enemy.

The journey south took several days. Fortunately the chieftain of the savages exhibited strong leadership qualities, and the women and children were treated respectfully. She shuddered to think of what might happen if he allowed the warriors to run wild among the prisoners.

The trek became more difficult as they pushed through the barren hill country. Each night they settled in a lonely country spot. The women were allowed to gather firewood, and at the end of each day several animals from the herd were driven in for them to butcher and cook. Water was plentiful, and they devised a way to carry water to see them through the long days of travel.

The cold nights caused suffering, until Abigail organized them in groups to huddle together around small fires. But they survived, despite fatiguing hours of trudging through rugged country and the despair which gripped every woman and child. It took all of Abigail's strength and resolve to encourage her army of prisoners, in addition to caring for her own son.

Ahinoam was no help. She seemed almost to give up. She fed her baby without the cheerfulness she had once shown; her moans and complaints set a bad example for the other mothers who faced the same hardships. She taxed Abigail's patience. Only by constantly reminding her that she was responsible for David's heir could Abigail keep Ahinoam from giving up completely.

An Amalekite slave had been assigned to the prisoners to make sure their needs were met. Every evening when they camped, he drove in a few goats or sheep or cattle and helped them with the slaughter and cooking. Abigail decided to befriend him.

The boy was barely in his teens, as ragged and dirty as the other Amalekites. His beardless face was filthy; his long matted hair smelled of manure. When Abigail spoke to him, he only muttered a few unintelligible words and turned away.

"He speaks Egyptian, Mother Abigail," whispered Neferah bath Heleb, wife of one of David's warriors. She had been born in Egypt.

"Speak to him, then," said Abigail. "Learn his name."

Neferah and the slave boy talked briefly, then the woman turned to Abigail and said, "His name is Tutamon. He has been an Amalekite slave since he was a child, when his Egyptian parents sold him into slavery."

"Talk to him some more," whispered Abigail. "See if you can gain his confidence. He may be helpful to us some time in the future."

And so a friendship grew between Neferah and Tutamon. She mothered him, and the boy responded.

As the relationship grew stronger, Abigail instructed Neferah. "Tell him to escape and return to Ziklag. There he must wait for David to return. Then David will know what has happened to us and will come to rescue us. Tell him he'll be well rewarded."

Neferah quickly agreed, seeing this as their best hope to be saved from future slavery, which she envisioned with all kinds of horrors. *Her fears are justified*, mused Abigail. Their plight was desperate, and they must do something soon or be lost forever.

The next night a different Amalekite slave drove the livestock into the women's camp. Abigail wondered if the boy had escaped, or maybe been caught and killed. There was no way of knowing, but hope soared among the women prisoners. They needed something to keep up their courage.

The trek southward took almost a month. It was not the driving of the flocks and herds which slowed the pace, but the women. They found excuses to delay: a sick baby, a lame child, fatigue—anything to slow the progress. The Amalekites shouted at them and sometimes beat them with sticks, but Abigail noticed that they did nothing to injure their prisoners. To save them for distribution later, she guessed. Again she was impressed with the leadership ability of their chieftain, as well as horrified by thoughts of their future.

Abigail tried to guess when David would be able to rescue them. How long would the war against King Saul take? A year? That would be too late. By then the women would be distributed and absorbed, probably impregnated with Amalekite seed and bearing their children. And there was no assurance that the Amalekite slave Tutamon had escaped alive and reached Ziklag. The city would be burned and destroyed; how would he survive while waiting for David to return home? The chance of their being rescued in time was slim, but she held to it.

In spite of her fears, she continued to show a cheerful demeanor. Any day now, she told the women, David's men would attack their captors and rescue them. Any day. David's army was in hot pursuit.

It was a lie; she knew it. There was little chance of rescue. They were doomed to a life of slavery. There was no way to avoid a devastating future.

Unless . . . unless Yahweh truly was with them!

The thought bolstered her courage. She was the wife of Yahweh's Anointed. Yahweh, David insisted, was with him in a special way. A dynasty would be established through his descendants. The House of David. Future generations, he insisted, would turn to the House of David for leadership and blessings. That was the eternal promise, given to their father Abraham so many generations ago. Yahweh would keep his covenant.

Abigail looked around at the bedraggled group of prisoners, weak from long travel, discouraged by thoughts of a dismal future. Doubts assailed her. Not even Yahweh could overcome the onrushing avalanche of fate. They were doomed.

Please, Yahweh, show us your strength now. Give us courage. And bring us your salvation. Before it's too late.

71

11

"OH, MOTHER ABIGAIL, what shall we do? How can we go on?"

Ahinoam's wail contained the despair of someone who had completely given up. Abigail took small satisfaction in being addressed "Mother Abigail" since it reflected what everybody in the large company of women had been calling her. Everyone—even Ahinoam—now recognized her as the "First Wife."

Abigail made an attempt to steady her voice. "Any day now, David and his men will come. Be looking for them."

She knew it wasn't true, but the words soothed the women who listened. Abigail herself had given up hope, but she tried not to show it.

"When?"

Abigail sighed. She had been through this same litany often during the past few days.

"That Egyptian slave boy, Tutamen, escaped four weeks ago, about a week after we were captured."

He probably didn't escape alive. The Amalekites surely killed him.

"If it took us a week to travel that far from Ziklag, it would take him only a few days."

But he's only a boy. He couldn't survive in this wilderness.

"Then in two or three weeks our men should return."

More likely a year.

72

"David and his men will leave immediately to follow us. They will travel this whole distance in a few days. That should put them here any day now."

That would be impossible. Miraculous, in fact.

"Don't forget, David is Yahweh's Anointed. God is with him in a special way. You, Ahinoam, hold in your arms the heir to the throne of Israel. Believe it. David will come."

Believe it. Believe it. You may, if I keep saying it often enough. Believe it. But do I?

They had arrived at their destination, a lonely oasis in the Negeb far beyond the southernmost Israelite settlements. Evidently it had been the Amalekites' starting point before the raid, because they joined their families there. The oasis was not large enough to support this many people and livestock, which meant they would be distributing the prisoners and spoils just before dispersing.

Soon. Very soon. Right after their celebration.

The men were celebrating now. Large quantities of captured wine had been opened. The warriors attacked the carefully hoarded beverage with a recklessness which showed their unfamiliarity with strong drink. Would their chieftain be able to control them? Or was he too drunk?

Abigail shoved aside her despair as she realized how close they were to being divided among their captors—or worse, ravished in a drunken orgy that very night. She must do something. Now.

They needed to be out of sight of the men. It might not help much, but if the warriors didn't see them, they might forget them in their drunkenness.

All the booty had been stacked near the women, probably for distribution tomorrow when the men recovered from their celebrations. Maybe the women could make themselves invisible there.

"Hide yourselves," she told them. "Over there, among

the baggage. Find blankets. Keep out of sight. If they don't see us—"

"But Mother Abigail, it won't stop them. If they don't find us tonight, they will tomorrow."

"We may be rescued by tomorrow."

"Do you think so? How do you know?"

I don't know. Or rather, I'm pretty sure we won't be.

"Because Yahweh is with us. David is coming."

"When?"

"Tonight."

They might not believe her, but they did as she said. Several hundred women could not hide long, but the night was dark and their captors drunk. Their concealment might buy them one more night before . . . before. . . .

She didn't want to think about that.

The baggage containing wealth David had collected over the years covered a large area of ground. Some of it was still in wagons piled high with rich cloth, spices, glass vases, handcarved furniture, jewels, ornamental carpets, and tapestries. Perhaps even weapons.

Weapons!

Abigail was startled to find a sword in the wagon near where she had settled in for the night. An ornamental sword, of course. Jeweled hilt. Bronze blade, not iron. It looked rich but was of little value in battle against iron weapons. Nevertheless she took and kept it beside her.

Then she tried to compose herself. It would be impossible to sleep, knowing what awaited her when the men recovered from their celebrations. But if she could rest, perhaps she would have more strength to face the ordeal.

It was hard to relax, however, because the noise of the revelry grew louder. She told herself to ignore it, shut it out, concentrate on soothing thoughts. Her baby Daniel was beside her, sleeping peacefully. Daniel. Chileab. Either name was agreeable to her. "God has judged." "Like his father." Good names. Honorable names. Names for the son of a king. The son of Yahweh's Anointed. Yahweh's Anointed.

The sounds of celebrations grew even louder. Different sounds. Shouts and cries and screams. That was no happy festival. Something was happening.

She arose and picked up her baby. Then with the ornamental sword still clutched in her hand, she went to the edge of the piles of plunder. She peered into the darkness, toward the large fire near the pond created by the spring in the oasis where the Amalekites were carousing. She could see them in the dancing firelight, figures running, leaping, fighting—fighting? What was happening?

Suddenly she knew! The Amalekites were being attacked. Attacked by an enemy, and that enemy was—

David!

"Praise Yahweh!" she shouted, and waved the ornamental sword.

Other women gathered around her. As realization dawned on them, they too began to shout. Some fell to their knees, weeping and praying. Others embraced, crying and shouting at the same time.

David had come! Yahweh's Anointed had saved them!

Suddenly Abigail froze. There, coming toward them, was a man. An Amalekite. He staggered. In the moonlight she could see that his face was bloody. He held a knife.

She recognized him then. He was the chieftain, who had controlled the Amalekites so forcefully on the trek south. Now his eyes blazed. Even in the darkness, she could see the steady purpose in his face as he plodded toward them.

He had come to kill them!

The women saw him too; they cringed back into the stacks of baggage behind them. Only Abigail, clutching her baby, stood her ground, facing him.

She could not move. She would not move. She was angry. The fear was gone. The exhilaration of rescue had displaced the horror of despair, and in its place was a cold fury. Rage—rage against this man, against all Amalekites.

One hand clasped her son tightly to her. The other hand held the ornamental sword.

In the days and years that followed, she could not remember clearly what happened in those intense moments. She would recall one scene, and one scene only. The chieftain lay on the ground, the sword embedded in his stomach. Dead.

Had she killed him? She would never know. Yahweh had mercifully erased those moments from memory.

12

THE REUNION between David and his wives was touching and tender.

Ordinarily Israelite men show no emotion in public toward wives, but David embraced them. Tears rolled as he poured out to Abigail and Ahinoam relief at finding them safe. He kissed his sons lovingly, showing no favoritism.

The strain of the past few weeks showed on his face. His usually cheerful countenance had become lined and darkened. Ordinarily a well-groomed man, he was dirty and sweaty, hair and beard untrimmed and unoiled. He spoke sharply to his men as he gave orders, and the tears which came so easily to his eyes reflected his taut nerves.

But he couldn't relax. After a brief reunion with his family, he plunged into organizing for the return trip. Abigail saw little of him during the three days of preparation.

At last they departed to retrace their steps in the difficult journey back to Ziklag. Abigail was relieved to find the trek considerably easier this time. For one thing, the women and children rode in carts. They were provided warmer clothing for the cold nights, and slept under tents. On many occasions during the nights, their own husbands shared the tent with them, which cheered them.

The return journey took a month. This time the slow pace was due to the flocks and herds, rather than the deliberate stalling of the women prisoners. While the Amalekites had pushed the livestock as fast as possible, trying to put as much distance between them and any possible pursuers, the Israelites drove them slowly, making sure they had adequate pasture and water.

During the trip, Abigail learned from David and others what had happened to bring rescue so quickly.

"We returned to Ziklag just four weeks after we left," David told her. "You can imagine how we felt, finding the city burned and our families gone."

Abigail nodded. She could guess the depth of despair and heartache this return could cause—for all the men, who would have been looking forward eagerly to reunion with their families. Only later did she learn that the men were so distressed they threatened to kill David in their anguished search for a scapegoat.

"But why," she asked her husband, "did you return to Ziklag so quickly? Surely the war against King Saul was not that short."

David grinned, although his face otherwise remained grim. "Achish didn't want us. He sent us home."

"Then he didn't trust you after all."

"It wasn't Achish. It was the other Philistine lords. They thought we would turn on them when we faced our own people in battle. They were right; I wouldn't fight against the Lord's Anointed, and our men feel the same."

"So you don't know yet how the Philistine campaign against Israel turned out."

"No. I'm anxious to get back and find out."

From Shammah ben Agee, who visited his wife often during the homeward trek, Abigail learned the fate of the Egyptian boy, Tutamen, who had escaped from his Amalekite master to seek David and bring him to the rescue.

"We found the boy south of Besor Brook. We were already in pursuit. That young Egyptian wasn't much help, but he sure relieved us when he said you were all right."

Abigail breathed a sigh of relief. She was more fond of the boy than she had realized. "And was Tutamen all right? Had he escaped unharmed from the Amalekites?"

Shammah grinned. "He was hungry. Hadn't eaten in three days. Dumb kid didn't know how to survive without someone to feed him and wipe his nose. Yeah, he had no trouble escaping from his master. He pretended to be sick and wanted to rest, so the Amalekite—who was just as dumb as that fool kid—believed him. He told him to stay behind, then catch up when he felt better."

"Could he show you which way we were heading?"

"We didn't need to know that. The trail was obvious. That many people, baggage carts, livestock—we couldn't miss the trail. But when we came to the Amalekite oasis, the kid was finally some help to us. He was familiar with that area, so he was able to show us how to sneak up on them while they were celebrating."

A few days later, Tutamen visited the women and sought out Abigail and Neferah, the woman who spoken to him in Egyptian. The boy, as Shammah had observed, was not too intelligent. He needed mothering. And Neferah, who was childless, took him under her wing.

They need each other, mused Abigail. Soon he would learn the Israelite language, and eventually be absorbed into their culture, finding life among his new masters much more pleasant than his previous existence.

At the end of a long exhausting trip, they arrived home. Home. The burned-out ruins of Ziklag.

Although Abigail knew the city they now called home had been destroyed, she wasn't prepared for the emotional shock the sight presented. She felt like an orphan. Obviously the other women felt the same, judging by the wailing and groaning around her.

"What shall we do?" she asked David.

"Yahweh will show us," he replied.

Always a pious answer. Abigail pouted. Even in the worst moments of despair, her husband's faith was deep. Ordinarily she would appreciate this. But not today. On the day she confronted her homelessness and uncertain future, she could not share her husband's faith.

But Yahweh did show them what to do. Only later did she come to appreciate the timeliness of what occurred next.

Reports began to filter in about a momentous battle in Israel, somewhere in the area of Mount Gilboa to the north. The Amalekites, they said, had completely destroyed the Israelite army. There were some reports that King Saul was dead, others that he and his son Jonathan had escaped. Nobody knew.

Until the Amalekite arrived.

David's lieutenant Joab brought the Amalekite to David while he was having lunch with Abigail. She watched as Joab cruelly forced the prisoner to his knees.

"The only reason I didn't kill him was because he was carrying this," Joab said. He handed David an ornate helmet and an armband. Both were made of iron, overlaid with gold and encrusted with jewels.

David gasped. "Where did you come from?" he demanded, pointing to the helmet and armband.

"Sir," the man replied from his prostrate position on the ground, "I brought them from the battlefield."

"What happened?" David's voice became sharp. "Tell me how the battle went."

Abigail frowned. Other survivors of the battle had appeared before David in the last few days, but none had evoked the reaction this man did. Perhaps it was the helmet and armband.

"Sir." The man seemed to gain confidence. He straightened to a kneeling position and looked David in the eye. "Our entire army was routed. We—"

"Whose army?"

"Er . . . ours. The Israelites. I am a servant of King Saul."

"You say the Israelites were defeated?"

"Yes, sir."

"How badly?"

"Thousands of our men were killed or wounded. They—"

"And the king? And his son?"

"Dead."

"How do you know?"

The man hesitated, then continued. "Sir, I was there. On Mount Gilboa. I saw Jonathan fall. Then I saw the king. He leaned on his spear as the Philistines were closing in on him. He was wounded. And he spoke to me."

"What did he say?"

"He asked me to kill him. He was in great pain, and he wanted to be dead when the Philistines arrived.

"And?"

"So I killed him. I brought his crown and armband."

Abigail gasped. The man—an Amalekite—actually admitted killing Yahweh's Anointed. Before David. He didn't know how David felt about that. Perhaps he thought he would be rewarded.

David stared at the Amalekite for several seconds. Then he grasped his tunic and tore it from his neck to his waist. He burst into tears.

David's men who stood nearby also tore their clothes and began to wail. Abigail wondered how sincere their mourning was. But they followed David's example to mourn the passing of Yahweh's Anointed king and his son Jonathan.

All except Joab, whose face was grim. He grasped the Amalekite by his garment, yanked him to his feet, and led him away. Abigail could guess the man's fate.

For three days they mourned the death of the king and his heir. During that time David composed a dirge which he sang before his men. He roved the camp, playing his harp and singing his grief. Soon all the men were humming or singing snatches of David's lament, although Abigail was not sure of their sincerity. Saul was their enemy, the one obstacle to the throne of Israel. Now the obstacle had been removed. It was difficult to grieve this loss.

But David was sincere. What impressed Abigail most was not his grief over the death of Yahweh's Anointed but over the passing of the king's son. She had heard about the close ties of friendship which bound these two. David loved Jonathan like a brother—perhaps even more. David's own brothers were a part of his army, but he showed no more affection toward them than the other warriors. For Jonathan he mourned deeply.

Abigail shook her head in bewilderment. Her husband was filled with contradictions. He sought an end to the tyranny of King Saul, yet he grieved at his death. He loved his friend Jonathan more than his own brothers. He was tender toward his own family and solicitous toward his men, but cruel and savage toward his enemies. How could anyone who sang so beautifully have the ruthlessness needed to be king of Israel? Strange, strange were the ambiguities lurking in the mind of the man Yahweh had chosen to be his king.

At the end of the three-day period of mourning, David announced to his men what he planned. As he so often did, he couched his language in pious phrases.

"I inquired of Yahweh what we should do next. He told me to go to Hebron. There I will declare my kingship."

This brought an immediate and enthusiastic response from the men. "Hail to David, Yahweh's Anointed!

"David, mighty in battle, favored of Yahweh, wise in the councils of men, the fairest of ten thousand!

"Long live David, the new king of Israel!"

This last hail brought a frown to David's face. He held up his arms, and his forceful personality brought the cheers to a halt.

"We must be clear about this." He looked at the eager faces of his men. "I am not king of Israel. I am king of Judah. No more."

Cries of protest rose from the assembly. They naturally wanted their hero to succeed King Saul, since he had been specifically anointed by Yahweh to be the successor to the throne.

Abigail watched from a distance as the men tried to persuade him to fulfill his highest ambitions. Another contradiction, she thought to herself. David was a man spurred on by his ambitions. Everything he did was aimed at securing and reigning on the throne of Israel. Now, on the brink of fulfillment, he would settle for being king of only a small part of Israel. What next for her enigmatic, unfathomable husband?

Hebron. The largest city in Judah. Only a few years ago, it had been a large Canaanite center. Once it had been a city of the fabled Anakim, those giants of legend the mothers of Israel would tell their children about, saying, "The Anakim will get you if you don't behave."

The city had been conquered by Joshua and given to the people of Judah. To Caleb, specifically. That patriarch had settled there, and it had become one of the most powerful centers of Israelite population. It had even been chosen as a City of Refuge.

Now it would be Abigail's new home, only a few miles from Carmel, where she used to live. Abigail sighed.

Ruling Judah should be easier for her husband than ruling the larger kingdom of Israel. Perhaps David could live in peace. And, she hoped, so would she.

13

"OH, MOTHER ABIGAIL!" Ahinoam grinned, and her dark pretty face seemed to sparkle. "I am with child!"

Abigail paused in her kneading of the dough for the daily bread which must be ready for this evening's supper. She smiled, sharing Ahinoam's excitement.

"I am too," she said.

Ahinoam giggled. "Really? Wonderful! Yahweh be praised! I wonder which one will be born first?"

"Maybe they'll have the same birthday. Will that make them twins?"

Ahinoam chuckled. "I told David last night. He said it will be another boy."

"I'm not surprised. Our husband doesn't know his wives are capable of producing daughters."

Ahinoam's laugh echoed around the large courtyard, causing Amnon and Daniel, their four-year-old sons, to look at the their mothers seated at the table. *Happy, happy family*, reflected Abigail as she continued to work and laugh with her closest friend. *May it ever be this way. Please, Yahweh, continue to bless us with peace and happiness.*

Abigail wondered if the God she silently prayed to would heed a request from so lowly a person. Perhaps if this prayer were offered by Yahweh's beloved—her husband—it would have a better chance of being answered.

But maybe not. God answered prayer according to his will, not theirs. And in his wisdom he always seemed to balance their lives with both good and bad experiences, enabling them to appreciate both.

She breathed deeply of the warm morning air, so soaked with sunshine and fragrance. Here in the broad courtyard of their spacious home in Hebron, four families lived together in harmony and happiness as the royal household of the kingdom of Judah.

When they had moved from Ziklag four years ago, the fawning citizens of Hebron had given them this large house on the hill. But Abigail knew their gratitude was not merely because of the generous gift David had given them from his wealth recovered from the Amalekites, but also because they recognized David's strength and bright future. Although he insisted on being king in Judah only, everyone knew that sooner or later he would rule all Israel. Yahweh had ordained it.

Abigail sighed. If only David were content to remain ruler of this small province, then their happiness could continue. But his ambition reached out, yearning for a greater destiny, the conviction strong within him that God had established his future. And his future included much more than this small, happy kingdom.

The house in Hebron was the largest Abigail had ever seen. Some said it had been built a hundred years before by Arba, the legendary hero of the giant Anakim people who lived there before Joshua and Caleb conquered the city. The royal house stood proudly on the highest hill, and from the rooftop one could see the broad Judean countryside, with its forested hills and valleys and pastures and streams. A fitting home for the royal Shepherd of Judah.

The house was so big four families lived there comfortably. Besides herself and Ahinoam, Miriam and Shua occupied the spacious rooms. Miriam, a jolly middle-aged matron, was married to Shammah ben Agee, whom Abigail had come to know at Carmel while waiting for her husband David to send for her. Miriam's children had grown and were now young warriors under Joab, David's commander-in-chief. And Shua, her young servant and companion, had married Hezro when they lived in Ziklag. Now they had two small children, a boy and a girl.

Abigail mixed nuts and honey into the wheat flour she had been kneading, then shaped it into four loaves which she placed in the sun to rise. By late afternoon they would be ready to bake in the oven in the corner of the courtyard. Tonight at supper the bread must be served hot, fresh, and aromatic. How many people would her husband bring home for supper tonight?

She busied herself with the daily household tasks. The day passed swiftly and happily. Even though her husband was king of Judah, she felt more like a common housewife waiting for her man to come in from the fields.

In late afternoon she checked the cauldron which simmered on the brazier next to the oven and added water to make sure it would not boil down too far. There must be enough for at least ten people. She stirred the thick mass of stew, which included goat meat and vegetables and several spices. She tasted the stew and added salt and coriander. She would be humiliated if the guests made unfavorable comments on the taste of the dinner at the king's table.

When David arrived, Abigail did a quick count. Six men would be served at the supper table on the roof tonight. Besides David, Shammah, and Hezro, who lived here, his guests would be the sons of David's sister Zeruiah—Joab, the commander-in-chief of David's armies, and his brothers, Abishai and young Asahel.

David refused to wear royal clothing except for state

occasions. Today he wore the short tunic and sandals of a soldier, much to the delight of his warriors. He greeted his family boisterously, planted token kisses on the cheeks of his two wives, then led the dinner party to the roof. There the setting sun would bring cooling breezes as well as give the men a spectacular display of color as it dipped behind the distant hills.

The four women served the meal. Abigail busied herself around the table supervising the serving of the food and did not leave the rooftop. She wanted to hear the discussion of the men, knowing that later she would herself discuss it with David after everyone had retired for the night.

Supper on the rooftop was the time David and his men mulled over the events of the day, planned strategy for the future, and made assignments for the next day's tasks.

"Who does Abner think he is?" demanded Joab loudly. "He has no right to speak for Ishbosheth."

Abigail bit her lip as she poured wine into Shammah's cup. She had followed their conversation from the moment they entered the gates of her house. The topic of their discussion was the messengers from the kingdom of Israel who had arrived today to propose a peace conference.

Ishbosheth ben Saul had been anointed king of Israel, the eleven tribes to the north. Their present capital was Mahanaim, beyond the Jordan. He was a weak king, a figurehead only. Everyone knew that Abner, the commander-in-chief, held the real power in Israel.

"He does, though," replied David. "And he seems to be offering us the olive branch. We should take it."

"Don't trust him," muttered Joab, but nobody paid attention to him. They looked to David, who was not only their ruler but acknowledged by all to be the wisest man among them.

"Tomorrow, Joab, I want you to take three hundred men and go to Gibeon where you will talk to Abner. Find out his terms. And don't offend him."

"Shouldn't you go yourself?" asked Shammah.

David shook his head. "A king can't negotiate with a commander-in-chief; only another high-ranking officer may do that. If his terms are reasonable, accept them. Peace is always preferable to war."

"I still don't trust him," responded Joab, his voice guttural and savage.

Abigail, from her position as silent server at the royal table, observed Joab fearfully. Here was a man who could cause her husband trouble. Ruthless and impetuous, he would not hesitate to disobey his king if he thought it in the best interests of Judah. His loyalty to David was not in question, just his judgment and fiery nature.

Later Abigail expressed her feelings to David when they were alone. "Don't trust your nephew Joab. You never know what he'll do."

"I know, my love." As always, David spoke tenderly, but she knew he listened to her. "I will tell Shammah and Hezro to stay close to him. They'll keep him out of trouble."

But Abigail wasn't so sure. Not even the moderating counsel of David's two trusted advisers could stem the impetuous and emotional commander-in-chief when he believed he was right.

The next day Abigail watched from the rooftop as Joab led four hundred men out of the north gate of the city for the one-day journey to Gibeon. She didn't know whether to be grateful or unhappy because her husband was not with them. Such silly rules, that the king should not negotiate with a commander-in-chief. David—not the impulsive Joab—should deal with the cunning Abner. But at least Shammah and Hezro would be there. Their steady counsel should balance Joab's impetuosity.

Five days later they returned.

Abigail hurried to the rooftop to watch the sad procession which entered the north gate of Hebron. They carried stretchers. Abigail shuddered. The stretchers carried bodies.

She could hear the wailing but not the words spoken to David who met them at the city gate. She could see David tear his clothes and sprinkle dust on his head. Whether it was victory or defeat, he would mourn the men lost in battle.

Battle! There should never have been any battle. This was a peace mission. Her forebodings had been accurate; Joab had gone to Gibeon seeking war, not peace. Not even Shammah and Hezro could stop him.

There would be no supper for her household tonight.

The day was early enough that they could bury the dead before sundown, but the period of mourning which followed would be a period of fasting. And silence. They could not speak until sundown, and Abigail knew her husband would enforce this custom rigidly, because his mourning was sincere.

Only David, Shammah, and Hezro met on the rooftop that night. Joab and the others had gone home, to mourn the dead in their own way.

As the shadows stole across Hebron and the sun slipped into its colorful home in the western hills, Abigail stood silent and unmoving in a corner by the parapet of the rooftop. The city below her was quiet, the people—like David—mourning the dead.

Just as the last fiery tip of the red sun dipped behind the distant hill, David spoke. "What really happened?" he demanded.

Shammah sighed. "We fought," he said simply.

David waited. Shammah would tell it in his own way.

"We arrived at Gibeon at sundown." Shammah's voice, usually boisterous and loud, was now soft and subdued. The aura of mourning still pervaded the men on the rooftop.

"We immediately went into camp at the edge of the pool. Abner and his men were already there, encamped on the other side."

Abigail pictured it in her mind—Abner and his men encamped against the wall on one side of the pool; Joab and his soldiers on the other. The pool was man-made, cut into the rock just inside the city wall. The spring which bubbled up gave the residents an unfailing water supply in time of siege.

"In the morning, we talked. Across the pool. Abner proposed a contest. Swordplay. Twelve young men from each side."

David nodded, and Abigail understood. This was a peace conference, and the brief display of swordplay was meant as sport, with no bloodshed. A common enough form of entertainment in any gathering of warriors.

"But Joab instructed our men to kill."

Abigail gasped. David frowned.

Shammah continued. "Hezro and I tried to stop them, but Joab demanded we get out of the way. He was the commander-in-chief; what else could we do?"

David nodded again.

Shammah went on. "It was a bloody encounter. All of Abner's young men were killed. So were ours. Even with surprise on our side, Abner's youths were somehow able to respond. It was . . . it was. . . ."

"Ghastly," supplied Hezro.

Shammah drew a deep breath and continued. "Then Joab gave the order to attack. Abner gave the order to retreat. They fled out the gate and ran into the hills. We followed."

Abigail gripped the edge of the parapet. So Abner had enough good sense to run. He wasn't cowardly, not Abner. The old warrior had proven himself on the battlefield too often for any one to believe that. But he was a shrewd old man. Fighting at this time would accomplish nothing. Abner had come to Gibeon for peace, not war.

"We followed. Joab instructed his men to kill, and they did. A lot of Abner's men fell that day."

David's face was grave. He knew the deaths would not be forgotten. Retaliation, blood revenge, would follow.

"Then we found Asahel."

Shammah's voice faltered. This tough old warrior, so inured to battle, could scarcely continue. But he mastered himself and went on. "Abner's spear was in his belly. Joab and Abishai stopped only a moment, looking down at their younger brother. Then with a savage cry, they ran after Abner, shouting curses and cries of vengeance."

At this point in his narrative, Shammah could not continue. Tears streamed down his cheeks.

Hezro took up the story. "I knelt down beside Asahel. He was still alive. Joab and Abishai had not even stayed to find that out. But the boy was able to gasp out the story of what happened."

Hezro's eyes met David's, and his voice hardened. "Abner had warned him to leave off pursuit. He didn't want to kill the brother of Joab."

Abigail's fingers gripped the parapet. Shrewd old Abner. He knew the consequences of angering the fiery Joab.

"But Asahel continued to press the attack. And Abner thrust his spear into Asahel's stomach." Again Hezro paused in his narrative.

His next words were cold and ominous. "Butt first."

David impulsively tore his already ragged tunic. He would know what Hezro meant. So did Abigail. Abner did not try to kill the boy, only stun him. And stop him.

"But the spear butt pierced Asahel's stomach. We could do nothing. He died there in my arms."

David listened intently as the rest of the story poured out from Shammah and Hezro. Abner had escaped, but many of his men had not. Most of them, in fact. They lay dead on the road that passed through the plain of Gibean.

Joab and his men, after Abner's escape, took Asahel's body to Bethlehem, where they buried him in the tomb of Aruiah, their father. Then they returned home to Hebron.

Later David stood beside Abigail by the parapet on the rooftop, looking out over the silent city.

"War," he muttered. "War with Abner."

Abigail's heart went out to him. Her husband was a man of war, mighty in battle, skilled as a leader of men. But he was still a man of peace, who hated war.

Civil war at that. War against their own brothers. All of them children of Abraham. Together they shared the eternal promise.

David sighed. Abigail wondered if their thoughts ran parallel at that moment. The promise: that through the children of Abraham, all the people on earth would be blessed. But how could that be, if they fought each other?

Ahead were days of agony and anguish. And death. The deaths of many promising youths, cut off from life before they could taste some of their best years.

War. The way of death. And because of Joab, David's commander-in-chief. Because of his savagery, they must all suffer.

14

DURING THE next year, Judah and Israel clashed several times, mostly because Joab enthusiastically embraced the idea of war. Impetuous and belligerent, he seemed restless and unhappy in times of peace.

David attempted to restrain him, trying to direct the energies of his bellicose commander-in-chief toward some of the hostile Canaanites in the south. Several times Joab led his men out of Hebron on the road to the south, only to return a few weeks later from the north, having circled around to attack some unsuspecting town or prosperous rancher in Israel.

David rebuked him, but it did no good. Joab was too independent and too confident of his security as David's kinsman and chief officer.

"Why don't you replace him as commander-in-chief?" asked Abigail one night when she and David were alone. They had retired to David's rooftop sleeping chamber for the night. This was the time she and her husband could talk alone.

David shook his head slowly. "He's my nephew," he muttered.

"Sometimes I think he's your enemy," she replied.

David grunted. "Never that. He's the most loyal man in Judah. I can't reward fidelity with demotion. His methods are different from mine, but our objectives are the same."

"You both want to see you seated on the throne of Israel, right?"

David nodded.

Abigail pressed on. "But you don't want to reach that throne by wading through a river of blood. And Joab thinks the shortest road to the throne is by adding to that river, most of it dripping from his sword."

David laughed softly. "You have a way with words, my love. But yes, that about describes it. I'll wait for Yahweh to give me that throne, peacefully, and with the good will of the people of Israel. When he does, my rule will be a lot smoother."

"My husband is wise." Abigail touched his hand. "And farsighted. If only you didn't have a blind spot where your nephew is concerned."

David pulled his hand from hers and placed it on her swollen stomach. "Here's one person who is more important to me than Joab. Daniel is another." He gazed fondly across the sleeping chamber, where their five-year-old son lay sleeping peacefully. "And Amnon, and all the other sons who will be born to me in future. And their sons. And all the young men who will be born in the years ahead. The House of David."

His words were spoken softly; Abigail sensed the depth of his feeling. He saw clearly the promise God had spoken to Abraham, that these people whom Yahweh had chosen would grow, become strong, and be a blessing to all mankind. David saw this promise as something more personal, more narrow than just the multitude of Abraham's sons. To him the promise would be fulfilled in the sons of David.

Two weeks later, Ahinoam's baby was born. A girl.

David's disappointment moderated as he turned to Abigail, whose time for delivery had almost come. "At least I have another chance for a third son," he muttered.

But Abigail also brought forth a girl.

When David learned the sex of the child, he left the house abruptly and sought solitude on a nearby hillside. The women informed Abigail of his silent departure.

"He was frowning," said Shua, who had watched him leave. "I don't think he was happy about your giving him a daughter."

Abigail cradled the tiny new infant in her arms, and the hungry mouth sought her breast.

"He needs sons," she murmured. "After all, he's a king."

In spite of her attempts to justify her husband's attitude, she felt let down. This tiny innocent life, so delicately created by her husband and herself by a miraculous process established by Yahweh, was a precious gift, as precious and welcome as any boy would have been.

But she was a king's daughter. And a king needed sons.

David left the naming of his daughters to his wives. Ahinoam named hers Naomi. Abigail understood why. The name meant "Pleasant." Ahinoam basked in the pleasant life she led at Hebron. Wars might be fought, kingdoms wrested away from usurpers, young men die bravely on the battlefield while their families mourned, but inside the walls of David's house at Hebron, there was joy.

Abigail chose a different name for her daughter. Salome. "Peace."

Ahinoam liked the name immediately. To name David's daughters "Pleasant" and "Peace" seemed appropriate for their happy household. She had no appreciation of Abigail's yearning for her husband's kingdom to thrive without the bloodshed, the grieving over lost sons and husbands, the anguish felt by mothers and wives when their men marched off to war. She didn't care whether the kingdom her husband ruled was tiny Judah or magnificent Israel, as long as there was *peace*.

David's uneasiness over the birth of two daughters virtually at the same time prompted his next decision. "I plan to marry another wife," he announced to his wives one day.

Ahinoam's dark face grew even darker as she absorbed the news. She said nothing, however, because she was a dutiful wife. Abigail understood her feelings. She believed this decision might well disturb the "peace" and "pleasantness" of their happy existence.

Abigail, however, also understood her husband's reasons. He thought like a king. Not only did he need sons to establish his dynasty, but he also needed alliances. At first, as was the case with both her and Ahinoam, he needed wealth, and marriage was the quickest and least bloody way of attaining that. But now . . . now he was a king, he had to think of marriage in terms of political expediency.

And so, after much careful thought and planning, he married Maacah, daughter of Talmai, king of Geshur.

Geshur was a small kingdom east of the Jordan River. The political shrewdness of this move was its location, just north of Mahanaim, the capital of Israel. That was where Abner lived. And Ishbosheth ben Saul, who now ruled the Kingdom of Israel. They would be uneasy, living next to a nation which, however small, was allied to their enemy by marriage.

And Talmai, king of Geshur, was a strong and stubborn man. Abner and Ishbosheth would think twice before attacking him.

When Maacah arrived, she made an ostentatious entrance into the city of Hebron. She rode on an open chair, carried by twelve sturdy Geshurites and followed by a train of servants, bodyguards, and oxcarts laden with rich possessions. Only later did Abigail learn that she had stripped the small kingdom of much of its wealth to bring with her to her new marriage.

She also brought with her the haughtiness and demeanor of a spoiled princess. When she learned Abigail was first wife not by order of marriage but by David's appointment, she immediately sought to wrest that position away.

At first she attempted to overwhelm David with her charms. She was a beautiful girl with large expressive eyes and a flattering tongue which she used lavishly on her husband. But her request to take over the position of leadership in the household was rebuffed, causing pout lines to appear on her pretty face when she emerged from David's sleeping chamber on the roof one morning. All the women in the household guessed what had happened and were greatly amused.

The power struggle continued. Maacah was determined to be the queen of Hebron, in spite of David's rejection of her request. She gave orders to her servants to take over the duties of the household—the cooking, the making of garments, the arrangements for entertaining guests, and the dealing with merchants who came to the courtyard each day with their wares.

At first Abigail tolerated this. But when Maacah began to discipline and give orders to Amnon and Daniel, she knew the time had come to deal with the new wife.

Abigail chose the place for the confrontation carefully: the rooftop, just outside David's sleeping chamber. The specious rooftop held three sleeping rooms. The largest was occupied by David and his current conjugal companion; the other two by Shammah, Hezro, and their wives.

The day was cold, with a threat of rain. Clouds rolled up in the north, and occasional gusts of wind blew across the parapet. Abigail waited, ignoring the blustery weather.

And waited. Maacah chose to ignore Abigail's summons, or at least delay her response. When she finally arrived, she was dressed in a long purple cape—purple—and a gold crown on her head.

The most regal thing the new queen wore was her smile. She held her chin high, looking down on the low-born "other wife" with condescension and disdain. Abigail felt the chill. Fortunately she had chosen to wear a warm woolen cloak, which, though less dazzling than her rival's purple one, was warmer. It helped her endure the coldness of the other woman's gaze.

"Maacah," she greeted the girl. "Third wife of David, king of Judah."

Maacah's chin tilted even higher, if that were possible.

"Abigail." Maacah's voice matched the temperature of the wind. "Widow of Nabal and third wife of David."

The insult was deliberate and clever, showing her knowledge of David's family history. Not only was it a reminder that David had married the widow of a fool, but also that Abigail, not Maacah, was the third wife in chronological order if you counted Saul's daughter Michal, whom David had married first and never repudiated.

"Everyone knows," said Abigail, frost touching her voice, "that just because Michal is the daughter of a king, she is not first wife."

"Only because she isn't here." Maacah's rejoinder conveyed the unspoken implication: *But another king's daughter is here, and should be first wife.*

Abigail continued. "I have summoned you this morning because our house is too small. I must ask you to please dismiss your bodyguards and your servants and send them back to Geshur. You may keep three ladies of your choice. The others must return."

A small twitch of fear flicked across Maacah's face. Abigail smiled to herself. This cold princess wasn't as secure as she appeared. Only one thing remained to be said.

"I have already discussed this with King David. He agrees. You have three days to inform the officer and decide which three ladies you wish to retain."

Now Maacah's face dissolved. Although she tried to look haughty, tears came unbidden to her eyes. "You . . . you wouldn't. . . ."

Abigail stared at the girl, now shivering in her thin majestic robe. The crown, worn only on festive occasions, had slumped at an angle on her head. Those regal shoulders seemed to sag. Abigail had won.

Suddenly Abigail felt a surprising surge of sympathy for this child. She was only sixteen, far from home, in a hostile household she couldn't control. Now her companions were to be sent home.

Abigail's voice softened. "I suggest, my dear, that you accept the reality of your situation. As soon as you receive David's seed in your body, you will be sleeping in the long room below, with the rest of us. You need us. We can be . . . your friends, if you'll let us."

She smiled, trying to convey as much warmth as she could on this chilly rooftop. "And I want to be your friend. Please. Let me."

But habits of a lifetime could not be so quickly shattered. Maacah took a deep breath, trying to master herself and regain some of her aloofness. "Is that all, Mother Abigail?" she asked, her voice strained.

Abigail nodded; the girl turned away. Maybe she had requested an end to the interview because she was cold. More likely she needed time to think. To retreat to a secluded place and regain her composure. Perhaps cry a little. And accept defeat.

But she has already accepted that, reflected Abigail. Her last words were addressed to "Mother Abigail." So different from her caustic opening words in the confrontation: "Abigail. Widow of Nabal and third wife of David."

Abigail felt no sense of triumph as she mulled over the interview. She had won, yes. But that was no victory, because her position as first wife had already been established beyond vulnerability. She could not be deposed; her only victory was enabling Maacah to accept it.

And Maacah had. Now all that remained was to offer the hand of friendship.

Long after Maacah had gone down, Abigail remained on the rooftop. She hugged her heavy cloak around her and even welcomed the icy blasts which swept over the city. They seemed to clear her mind and bring her a new vision of her role as first wife.

When she was a child, her father had employed a Levite in his household to teach his sons the law of Moses. They had listened dutifully, although they were not much interested. But Abigail was. Often she had sneaked into the room where the Levite recited in a droning voice the sacred story, including both the history of Israel and the Mosaic Law. It had fascinated her.

The cold wind seemed to blow several particular passages of the sacred story into her mind. She could even recall the sound of the Levite's monotone voice as he droned. "When Yahweh brings you into your Promised Land . . . do not intermarry with the Canaanites, nor let your sons and daughters marry their sons and daughters."

Until Maacah came into their household, David had obeyed that law—since she, Ahinoam, and Michal were Israelites. But Maacah was the daughter of a Geshurite. Would there be more foreign wives?

In the voice of the wind, she seemed to hear the Levite's words as he recited another statement from the Law. This too reminded them of the time when they settled into their Promised Land. Some day they would choose to be ruled by a king. There were several admonitions for the king, and among them was this one: "He must not have too many wives, lest his heart be turned away from Yahweh."

Abigail shivered, but not from the cold. Was David

breaking the Law, flying in the face of express command-
ments from Yahweh?

She recalled one of her favorite passages from the sacred story, the opening drama about Adam and Eve's idyl-
lic life in the Garden. One man . . . and one woman. God
had set before his people an ideal for marriage, not by precept but by the example of the first-created man. "It is not
good that a man should live alone," Yahweh had said.
"Therefore I will create a companion suitable for him."
And he made Eve.

Adam. "The man." Eve. "Mother of life." The two became one. And Yahweh saw that it was good.

The people of Yahweh had by long tradition ignored
the ideal set by Yahweh, of one man and one woman, married, living together for life. Wealthy men had often taken
two or more wives and occasionally concubines. Kings of
other nations did it to ensure their dynasty. King Saul had
done it. And David was only being kingly by adding to his
royal household.

But had he gone too far by taking a foreign wife? Was
he creating a situation which would bring him troubles in
the future? Only Yahweh knew.

Abigail shook her head sadly. She knew she could not
say anything to David about this. To do so would sound
selfish and jealous. Besides, nothing could be done about
it now.

But there was something that could be done. They
needed a larger house. With a household growing ever
larger—even after several of Maacah's retinue had been
sent home—they needed more space. She resolved to
speak to David about this.

She had her chance the next morning. David lingered
in the courtyard to discuss with her the special guests he
planned to invite to supper. She agreed to send for a bull
to be slaughtered for the meal.

With that out of the way, Abigail brought up the subject of overcrowding. "My lord husband, I told Maacah yesterday that you had ordered her to send home her bodyguard and some of her personal handmaids."

"How did she take it?"

Abigail shrugged. "She didn't believe me. I told her to check with you."

David grinned. "Yes, she asked me last night. I told her it was my idea."

Abigail grinned back at him. It had been her idea, and he knew it. That was the reason for the grins.

"Even so," continued Abigail, "this household is too large for this house."

"It's the biggest house in Hebron, my love."

"So it is." Abigail smiled shyly, looking up at her husband. "Could we have a second house?"

"How would you like it if I built you a palace?"

"I'd love it. When will you start?"

David touched her hand gently. "Not yet, I'm afraid. I want to build a Temple first, a house for Yahweh before a house for myself. And I don't want to build it here in Hebron."

"Not in Hebron? But why not?"

"Hebron is Judah's capital. We should have a capital north of here, which would not reflect favoritism for either Judah or Israel."

"But wouldn't a northern capital favor the northern tribes? How will Judah feel about that?"

David smiled at her. "You understand politics better than most men. And you're right. We must have a neutral capital, one that doesn't belong to either kingdom."

Abigail stared at him. "Then . . . you're going to conquer a new city. Aren't you? Some place like Jerusalem?"

David laughed. "How shrewd you are, my love. You've already guessed my plans."

"But Jerusalem is impregnable. Those walls. . . ."

David nodded. "Yes. In fact, the Jebusites who live there have taunted us. They tell us that even the blind and the crippled could defend their city successfully. They're right about that as far as the walls are concerned. They're strong, but treachery can bring down any city."

"Treachery?"

David nodded. "Treachery. We already have a defector from the Jebusites. He has promised to show us a way into the city."

"How?"

"Through the water tunnel. Their main source of water comes from a pool outside the city walls. The tunnel leads from the pool directly into the heart of the city. It's a carefully guarded secret."

"But not carefully enough . . . if there's a defector."

"Right, my love. Joab will lead a surprise attack soon."

"Joab." Abigail frowned. "Yes, that sounds like his kind of work."

David laughed. "You never did like him, did you?"

She shook her head. "No. He will cause you a lot of trouble in the future."

"Nobody in all Israel is more loyal than Joab."

Abigail said no more. She could never persuade David to separate himself from his beloved nephew and trusted commander. She hated to think what he might do to his king in the future.

But she must not think about that. Not now. Not with the exciting prospect of a new palace, which her husband would build for her as soon as Jerusalem was conquered.

A palace. A big one, bigger than their present home. Big enough to contain all David's wives. And more to come. More wives . . . and, no doubt, more trouble.

15

JOAB BROUGHT HOME David's next wife not long after.

He had been raiding in the north, in the valley of Elah, among the prosperous families of the Benjamin tribe in Israel. He brought home a wealthy widow—whose husband, if the rumors were true, was murdered by Joab himself.

For several days a procession approached Hebron. Cattle, sheep, goats, even a few camels and horses were included. They were shunted into the broad pasture south of Hebron, where they joined other herds owned by the now wealthy kingdom of Judah. Ox-drawn carts loaded with precious goods lumbered through the gates toward the warehouse where the goods would be distributed or sold. The already luxurious Judahite homes would be enriched by carpets, tapestries, hand-carved furniture, glass vases, fine clothing, and jewels.

Perhaps, mused Abigail as she watched the parade from her rooftop, that was why David's rebukes to Joab bore no sting. The raids prolonged the Judah-Israel war, but in the process Judah had waxed strong and glowed with wealth, while Israel weakened. In public, David lectured loudly about the need for peace with Israel, and Joab continued to ignore his protestations of pacifism. The king of Judah proclaimed peace while growing rich on war.

On the fifth day of the procession to Hebron displaying the wealth of the recent raid, Joab arrived—with the widow. He presented her to David. The king accepted her, and she became his fifth wife, Haggith.

The name meant "The Festal One." But she didn't look especially festive now, Abigail noted, as she met with the new bride on the rooftop.

Her robe, though worn for several days and showing signs of dirt, was made of finest linen, with several colors woven into the fabric. She wore shoes—not sandals—of fine leather showing traces of red coloring beneath the mud. And the headpiece! A cone-shaped veiled masterpiece hinted of Babylonian origins.

But Haggith's shoulders sagged. She wrung her hands. Her eyes, when not downcast, showed red rims which spoke of many tears recently shed. The pretty face seemed prematurely aged.

"How old are you?" asked Abigail, her voice gentle.

Haggith gave her a quick frightened glance before murmuring, "Fifteen."

Abigail nodded. No wonder this rich girl was so frightened and subdued. She had probably been forced into a loveless marriage just after arriving at puberty, then widowed a year or two later. She might even have witnessed the brutal murder of her husband, then been dragged away by a savage Judahite commander and presented to the enemy king as a bride—or concubine. In a week she had plummeted from a pampered life of luxury where people attended her and leaped to obey her commands, to serving as slave of someone she knew little about.

Haggith. "Festal One" indeed!

"Let me help you," said Abigail.

The child looked up at Abigail with wide eyes. Hope showed there. Desperate hope. A way to survive.

As Abigail gave orders for heated bath water to be prepared and new clothes provided, Haggith gave herself gratefully into her new mistress's care. A bond forged between the two—the frightened, lonely, traumatized child and the gentle, sensitive mother-like first wife.

Abigail smiled at the irony of the situation. She was only twenty-four herself, yet she was matriarch of the family. A king's family. A growing prosperous family which turned to her for leadership. That they all called her Mother Abigail reflected her position.

Even Maacah called her Mother Abigail and sought her friendship. Now impregnated with David's seed, the Geshurite princess had been displaced from the royal bedchamber on the rooftop and relegated to the long sleeping room below with the other wives. Her haughtiness evaporated. Although she retained a close association with her three serving girls, she made a genuine attempt to win the affection of her sister wives. Following Abigail's example, they accepted her warmly.

As the days passed, Haggith began to display why she had been named the "Festal One." She glowed. Her laughter and high spirits enlivened the household. Soon every one of the royal women sought her friendship.

Abigail suspected the main reason for Haggith's good cheer was David. Everyone he touched fell under his spell. He had the rare ability to know what pleased a woman. She had never known a husband who gave her so much tenderness and passion in the wedding bed.

When Haggith emerged from the sleeping chamber each morning, she displayed a euphoria all David's wives understood. They shared a common bond, and while Abigail was sure each yearned for their husband's warm embrace at night, they showed no jealousy. On the contrary, they merged into a close-knit harmonious family which made life in the household a joyous experience.

Abigail attributed this to David's personality and magnetism. She rejected the idea that she herself was responsible, setting a tone of harmony and good will which she enforced by example and precept. No. It was David's charm, she told herself. Nothing more.

Two more wives were added to the growing family. Abital and Eglah. Daughters of powerful Canaanite kings. They too were mere children whom Abigail took under her wing. She infused them with confidence, participated in teaching them the new language, brought them fully into the intimate family of women who shared David's life. In both cases they responded to David's charm with warmth and joy as they embraced their new life.

During the two years after Maacah's coming, the family grew in other ways. Children were born in the household. Mostly sons, as befitted the royal ambitions of Yahweh's Anointed. But daughters too. A dynasty suddenly burst on the scene of Yahweh's chosen people, a dynasty which showed signs of fulfilling the promise spectacularly.

But the promise was for all Israel, not merely Judah. Abigail, now convinced that Yahweh monitored and controlled the events of David's life, marveled at what was happening around her. She felt very much part of it. But it puzzled her that Yahweh intended only the small yet prosperous kingdom of Judah to grow stronger, while the main body of Israelites grew weaker. Surely Yahweh had more in mind than this!

She was right. During the seventh year of David's reign in Hebron, events quickly occurred which would change the shape of their history.

Rumors had reached them of the growing dissatisfaction in the north, as Israel struggled in a hopeless war with Judah. The king, Ishbosheth ben Saul, was neither popular nor strong. His commander-in-chief Abner held the real power in Israel. Then, so they heard, Abner and Ishbosheth quarreled.

These rumors were confirmed when three ambassadors arrived in Hebron—not from King Ishbosheth, but from Abner. He wanted peace.

David, as his custom was, received these ambassadors on the rooftop of his home. Abigail and the other women worked hard to prepare a suitable feast. As usual Abigail placed herself strategically in a corner to overhear their conversation.

The visitors ignored her, assuming she was no more than a serving maid, and spoke freely. "My lord Abner brings you his warmest greetings, mighty king. He extends to you the hand of peace."

"And Ishbosheth?"

The ambassador, who seemed to be the head of the delegation, shrugged. "He concurs," he replied casually.

"I see." David's soft voice, while containing its usual charm, also displayed his strength. "And Abner's terms?"

"You, not Ishbosheth, will be rightful king of Israel and Judah. You will be anointed by a prophet or priest of your choice, at a location of your choice. All the tribes of Israel will be present to pledge their allegiance to you. You may select whatever city you desire to be your capital. You and your sons will hold the scepter of Israel forever."

Be careful, David. From her watchful position in the corner by the parapet, Abigail watched the deliberations. She suspected there was more to the terms than that.

So did David, evidently. "And what else? What does Abner want for himself?"

The ambassador hesitated, probably startled by David's shrewd insight and suspicion that there would be more. He squirmed a little in his seat. "All my lord Abner asks is that mighty King David appoint him commander-in-chief of the combined armies of Judah and Israel."

As David stroked his chin with thumb and forefinger, Abigail easily followed the thoughts running through the mind of her husband. There would be both advantages and disadvantages to that appointment. It would displace Joab, the unpredictable and savage warrior who gave David so many problems—but might make a dangerous enemy of him. Yet the move would insure the loyalty of all the tribes of Israel, who respected and obeyed Abner. That in itself might prove problematic—giving an already powerful man more power.

How would David answer this dilemma? His answer caused Abigail to gasp with surprise and amazement.

"I accept your terms. But I have two conditions of my own. I will appoint Abner commander-in-chief and will accept the scepter of both Judah and Israel only if you can guarantee that no harm comes to the son of Saul. And also I require that my wife Michal, Saul's daughter, be restored to my household immediately."

Abigail was so confused and startled by his unexpected statement that she scarcely heard the ambassadors' response. They accepted David's terms readily, no doubt because the conditions were trivial compared to their victory in having David make Abner commander-in-chief.

But the second condition was not trivial to Abigail. Why? Why did David place so much importance on his marriage with Michal? She had been given to another man by her father, King Saul, undoubtedly as a pointed insult to the rebel David. Michal had lived with that man for seven years—in adultery, so David claimed. She might even have borne children by her new husband.

But now . . . David wanted her back? Why? Did he still love her? Did she still love him? Would she disrupt the harmony of their family? Would Michal consider herself first wife, thus initiating a new power struggle?

Shammah had described her as shrewish and acid-tongued. Already Abigail hated her, hated this intrusion into her well-ordered and happy life. Many things were about to change, and the change threatened her.

16

EVENTS MOVED quickly after that. Just one month later, Abner himself came to Hebron.

Abigail watched from her rooftop the long parade of dignitaries as they approached the city. Word had flown ahead of them. By now everyone in Hebron knew exactly who made up the procession.

First there was Abner himself. The wily old commander had decided to place his life into the hands of his former enemy, offer his pledge of fidelity, and allow David to have his way. David had sent him assurances of safety and guarantees that he would be given the post of commander-in-chief of all the combined armies. Joab, his rival for this rank, had been sent out on another raid to the south. Joab presumably knew nothing of these unfolding events.

After Abner came twenty stately men, riding donkeys as befitted their exalted position. They represented all the tribes of Israel. Like Abner, they had come to pledge their fealty to David. Also like Abner, they were no doubt seeking personal gain.

Only thirty warriors, a token bodyguard, accompanied the peace party. They were dressed ceremonially rather than for war. Red feathers waved in their helmets, and their brass shields shone in the sun as they marched in parade formation behind the ambassadors.

The last person in the parade of dignitaries was Michal.

Abigail saw at once that her grand entrance would not be nearly as grand as that of Maacah, the princess-wife from Geshur. Michal rode a donkey alone. She had no chair borne on the backs of slaves. No large retinue of women to serve her in her new home. No bodyguard. And no procession of carts overloaded with rich possessions.

Michal was alone. A solitary proud figure sitting tall and regal on her donkey.

Yet it seemed to Abigail that she dominated the whole parade. Instead of just tagging along at the end, she became the climax of the parade, as though everyone who had passed before was merely the introduction to the finale. Even the donkey she rode strode proudly, slowly, deliberately, bearing with regal dignity the majestic figure of the new queen of Israel—David's first wife.

No. Abigail shook her head and clenched her teeth. She, not Michal, was the first wife—by appointment. The king himself had so decreed. Then why did she have to tell herself that? Why did she feel so threatened? What was there about that solitary figure in the distance that commanded attention and exuded power?

But Abigail had no time to spare for such thoughts. The peace party would be lavishly entertained that night on this very roof. Preparations had reached the frantic stage, when the careful planning and cooking and organization begun several days ago neared the climax. The broad rooftop contained many tables, covered with fine linen, and graced by the finest imported plates, bowls, and pitchers.

At sundown, torches were lit as darkness settled upon the city. Now it would be up to Abigail to oversee the serving of their guests, to make sure the meat was flavored properly, the bread fresh and fragrant, the freshly picked fruit arranged in colorful bowls, the cheese finely cut and displayed, the newly cooked vegetables spiced adequately but not too much.

And the wine. David's wives would serve it, after they had washed the feet of the ambassadors. Abigail herself planned to wash Abner's feet and serve his wine. Not only would this honor their most honored guest, but it would also give her an opportunity to overhear the conversation, which she wouldn't miss for anything.

Meanwhile, what would Michal be doing while all this frantic activity focused on the rooftop? Abigail shrugged. She would find out later. It might do the newcomer good to realize that the party upstairs—not her—was the focus of attention on this festal night.

The guests arrived at sundown. They were seated at tables, honored by the ceremony of foot washing, and served wine in shining silver goblets. The food was brought in with impressive ceremony, just as Abigail had rehearsed it earlier that day.

As she poured wine into Abner's cup, she saw Shua by the stairway leading to the courtyard, a look of strained agony masking her normally pretty features. Shua beckoned, her hand looking ghostly in the torchlight.

After pouring wine into the cups of both Abner and David, Abigail unhurriedly and with dignity walked through the festive tables toward the stairway where Shua waited wringing her hands.

"What is it, Shua?" she whispered.

"Oh, Mother Abigail! You must come immediately! Down there—"

Abigail touched her arm. "Not now, Shua. Deal with it as best you can. Miriam will help. She'll know what to do."

"But Mother Abigail—"

"Shhh! Keep your voice down."

"It's . . . it's that woman!"

"Who?" demanded Abigail, her voice louder than she would have allowed Shua's. But she already knew Shua's answer.

"Er . . . Michal."

Abigail took a deep breath, resentment filling her. That the new member of David's household would take advantage of the most frantic time of the day and the preoccupation of the women with their tasks did not surprise her. That things were happening down below which she would have to deal with later when she was tired—even that could be handled in time.

What concerned her most was Michal. The new wife. Taking over. Whatever she was doing down there, she could do without interference from the busy household. Sneaky. Malicious. Clever. And only the beginning.

Abigail sighed. "Let her do it, Shua. There's nothing we can do now. We'll just have to deal with it later."

"But Mother Abigail. . . ."

"I'm sorry. I have to go now."

Abigail strode back through the tables to the empty wine cups of her husband and his honored guest. She frowned, aware her face was set in a grimace. Full wine cups were more important than dealing with the family crisis. She sighed again, causing David to look up at her, a concerned frown reflecting puzzlement. Abigail smiled brightly at him, and he turned back to his guest.

Abigail forced herself to hold her shoulders back, her chin up, and her spirits high. Already exhausted, she faced a monumental task after the banquet. The cleanup. Not the cleanup of the messy tables, spilled wine, supper garbage. That was the easy part.

The real mess downstairs was what troubled her most. And she didn't even know what the mess was.

The banquet dragged on. Many wine jars were opened, and the ambassadors grew louder, their voices sometimes raucous. David drank little and retained his dignity. The songs he sang to entertain his guests calmed them by their beauty and charm.

Abigail's duties supervising the activities of the women distracted her from the mysterious sinister events occurring downstairs. Just now important speeches were being given; Abigail listened intently. Abner pledged steadfast loyalty to David. The ambassadors offered firm assurances of support from each tribe in Israel. The question of what to do with Ishbosheth arose.

David settled it by decreeing that no harm come to him. "Yahweh's Anointed is inviolate; the king must be honored, and all the House of Saul respected."

"And deposed!" shouted a drunken ambassador.

"And exiled!" yelled another.

"No." David's calm voice drew their attention, and a silence fell on the assembly. "They shall be allowed to live in peace. And treated respectfully."

"But my lord David," spoke one, his voice ragged and strained from too much wine. "We insist you be anointed and given the scepter of Israel."

"So it shall be." David's steady voice continued to spread calmness in a situation which showed signs of becoming unruly. "But my anointing will be here—in Hebron. Ishbosheth may remain in Mahanaim—unharmed, and with honor."

It's a good thing Joab isn't here, thought Abigail. He would probably advocate assassination. No, he wouldn't. He wouldn't say anything. He'd just go do it.

But what would happen when Joab returned home?

As the party neared an end about midnight, Abigail put in motion her plan for sleeping arrangements for the guests. On the rooftop. The tables were cleared away while the men stood by the parapet under the stars. The floor was swept of garbage and sleeping mats brought out and unrolled on the rooftop. Fortunately the night would be warm and pleasant, and the ambassadors would sleep soundly after all that wine.

Then Abigail and her women retreated below. She almost wished she didn't have to go. She dreaded what awaited her downstairs. And she was so tired! But she did not find the chaos she expected.

Michal had closed and barred the door into the long sleeping room after ejecting everyone and everything. The children, briefly awakened and shunted outside, had been taken to one of the side rooms where they had finally been hushed and put to sleep. All the bedding and personal belongings of the women had been thrown onto the floor of the courtyard.

A bodyguard of thirty men stood outside the long room door. They stood in a long line, their red plumed helmets distorted and enlarged in the torchlight. Abner's bodyguard. They should be in the barracks now, but they were here. And obviously under Michal's orders.

The women looked to Abigail for guidance. What should she do? Rouse David to deal with it? Find Hezro in the barracks and call out some of David's warriors to drive out Abner's bodyguard?

No. She would do nothing to cause further disturbance. She would simply ignore the situation and deal with it in the morning.

She assured the nervous weary women that everything was under control. "You've done so well," she told them. "The party tonight was handled flawlessly, in spite of this . . . small problem. You deserve rest. Take your bedding and go to the side rooms, or just bed down here in the courtyard. Don't forget, we have to get up at sunrise to bake the bread for the men's breakfast."

"But Mother Abigail, what about—"

"Tomorrow." Abigail's voice was firm. "We'll deal with it tomorrow."

Grumbling, the women turned away to find their bedding and retire for the few hours remaining of the night.

Abigail herself sat down on a bench to rest. She leaned back against the wall. Just a few moments, she promised herself. Then I must think. Plan what to do in the morning. What to do after the breakfast bread has been baked. And Michal wakes up. And the bodyguard. . . .

The sun on her face startled her into wakefulness. The day had arrived, and she had slept in. Her body was cramped and exhausted, her back sore where she had leaned against the corner wall.

She looked around. Several pallets lay on the courtyard floor, their unmoving occupants deep in exhausted slumber. The men in Abner's bodyguard also slept, sitting against the wall or sprawled on the ground. Their bright red plumes were not so bright this morning.

Miriam slept on the pallet nearest her, a soft snoring sound indicating the depth of her fatigue. Abigail went to her and shook her gently.

"Wake up, Miriam. We must begin the baking immediately."

Fortunately Miriam was able to rouse herself and stumble over toward the oven in the corner. The fire had been carefully banked for the night, and she added fuel to bring the oven temperature up to the heat necessary for the baking. The loaves had already been prepared the day before; soon the courtyard was filled with the sweet aroma of fresh bread.

Then Abigail went to the officer of the bodyguard and awakened him. "Sir," she said softly, "If you and your men will be seated at those tables, I'll serve you fresh bread and cheese, and perhaps some fruit."

The officer, a young nobleman, stared at her. Abigail wondered what he had expected this morning. Certainly not this.

She smiled at him. "Soon the men on the rooftop will arise, and they will want breakfast. You may eat first. Refresh yourselves, and enjoy the hospitality of King David's royal house."

The other women had by then been prodded into wakefulness. They stumbled drowsily around the courtyard doing their chores. More bread went into the oven. Soon from the rooftop came the sound of voices. The bodyguard hastily finished their breakfast, donned their helmets, and stood at attention around the courtyard walls.

David and Abner came down the stairs together. They both looked fresh and rested. Abigail wondered if their looks were deceiving; were they as tired as the women?

David glanced around at the bodyguard. Would he wonder what they were doing there? No. His courtesy as a host brought forth his first words.

"Have these warriors been breakfasted?" he asked.

"Yes, my lord husband," replied Abigail.

Abner turned to David. "But what are they doing here? I told them to wait at the barracks."

David turned to look at Abigail, an unspoken question wrinkling his forehead. But Abigail busied herself at the table, slicing cheese.

Abner beckoned to the captain of the bodyguard, and he marched stiffly over to stand before him.

"Why are you here?" he demanded.

The young man smiled. He had obviously come from an important family and was not intimidated even by his commander-in-chief.

"You asked us to be sure the lady Michal is comfortable. We have been attending her, my lord."

"I see," replied Abner tentatively.

"And where is the lady Michal?" asked David.

"In there, sir," replied the officer, nodding toward the door of the long sleeping room.

David glanced around. He saw the steadily increasing

activity in the courtyard: women carrying bowls of fruit, baking bread in the corner oven, placing pitchers of water on the tables. More men were coming down the stairs from the roof, attracted by the smell of fresh baked bread. Some of them demanded wine, probably to ease their heads throbbing from too much wine last night.

Then David turned to Abigail. "Is everything all right, wife?" he asked gently.

"Everything is fine, my husband. We gave Michal the long room last night. To make her first night in the royal household a little more comfortable."

David stared at her for a long moment. His thumb and forefinger massaged his chin. "I see," he murmured. "I think. Is there . . . ah . . . anything I can do?"

Abigail smiled. "No, my lord husband. Everything is under control. May I offer you this piece of date bread? Fresh-baked this morning."

"Thank you." He grinned. "I believe you. Yes. Everything is under control."

Abigail bowed and turned to see to the needs of the guests. Her heart warmed toward David. Obviously he had guessed her dilemma. He understood. And he trusted her to handle the situation without interference.

Later, while the ambassadors were preparing to leave, David passed Abigail and briefly touched her arm.

"I'll see you tonight," he whispered. "Spend the night in my sleeping room. I want to talk with you."

Abigail's heart leaped. David had chosen her to be with him tonight. Her. Not Michal!

Her fatigue was forgotten. She almost floated as she supervised the cleanup after the men had gone. She smiled and even hummed a tune.

Now, she thought, glancing toward the closed door of the long sleeping room. *Now, Michal, crawl out of your hole. Anytime you want. I'm ready to deal with you!*

17

THE SUN HAD risen high when Michal finally unbarred the door and stepped into the courtyard.

Abigail at first was unaware of her entrance. As she swept the floor of the oven, some of the ashes and dust rose in a cloud and smudged her gown and face. She must wash her face and change her dress soon, right after the dirty part of the chores had been completed. Preferably before their pampered guest in the long room woke and made her appearance.

The sudden silence in the courtyard alerted her. She stood up and wiped her face, probably smudging it further. The door of the long room was now open; Michal stood in front of it in regal splendor.

She wore a long white dress, bound at the waist by a purple cord. Her hair, elegantly piled on top of her head, was crowned by a large golden tiara. A golden necklace graced her long neck. Makeup highlighted her lips and eyebrows. And she stood tall and majestic, like a queen surveying her domain.

Abigail dropped the broom immediately and walked across the courtyard toward her. The other women had drawn back, silent now, watching the drama about to be enacted on the courtyard stage.

Abigail smiled as she stopped before the imposing newcomer. "Welcome, my lady, to the royal household of

King David, ruler of Hebron and soon to be king of Israel. We trust you were comfortable last night?"

Whatever Michal had expected, it was not this. Her mouth dropped slightly and some of the stiffness went out of her.

But she instantly recovered and spoke in a chilling voice. "And who are you?"

"I am Abigail."

"I see."

Michal's eyes looked disdainfully at Abigail, measuring her from head to toe. Abigail struggled to keep her composure under those cold eyes, aware of her smudged face and dirty dress. She tried to hold her smile.

Michal's next words dripped contempt. "Abigail. Widow of Nabal, the fool. The third wife."

It was exactly as Abigail had expected. Michal's strategy would be condescension, standing in icy aloofness and looking down on the lesser creatures. Abigail's counter strategy would be composure, cheerfulness, and friendship.

"Michal," she replied, forcing her voice to contain warmth, with no hint of sarcasm. "Daughter of King Saul. David's first love. You are most welcome here."

Michal's eyes narrowed and her lips compressed, giving her face a hardened look. Obviously cordiality was not what she expected. Had she prepared herself to exchange insults, perhaps dueling verbally with her rivals, goading them to lose their composure and make them look foolish? Maybe. If so, she had not planned a counter-attack against civility.

"You may serve my breakfast now," she said.

"We have it ready for you, my lady." Abigail waved her open hand toward the table. "Bread baked this morning, cheese, several different fruits. What is your pleasure?"

"While I am eating, I want you to arrange to make adequate provision for my needs. I left in a hurry, and could not bring my servants and possessions with me. I will need at least five women to serve me, new carpets for my room, the finest furniture, and ten eunuchs to be my personal bodyguard."

Abigail struggled with herself a moment. She had almost laughed in the woman's face. Eunuchs! She had heard about unmanned men who served in a queen's retinue, in Egypt or Babylon or some of the other courts of distant lands. But in Israel such a servant was unthinkable. Even laughable.

"I will be sharing the bedroom of the king, of course," went on the haughty lady, "but I will retain this room as my own. It is barely adequate, but it will suffice."

Abigail paused a second before responding to make sure her voice was cheerful. It wasn't as difficult as she expected, since she was closer to laughter than to tears at that moment. She must speak respectfully as well as jovially, according to her strategy. But this woman was making it difficult to keep from laughing at her, which she did not want to do.

"Please understand, my lady, that we are very crowded here. The house is inadequate for our growing family. We have asked our lord King David many times for a new house, or at least a second house to shelter our people. He has promised us a grand palace, but not in Hebron. Patience, he counseled. And we are patient. You may keep the long room for a few days until you feel settled, but eventually we hope you will allow us to share it with you."

Abigail watched intently to see what effect her long speech would have on the newcomer. The sting had been withdrawn from the words by her smile and cordial demeanor, but the content of the words must surely pierce her heart. But if it did, Michal showed no indication. She stared at Abigail for a full moment before speaking.

"Go wash your face, child."

Then she turned and marched regally toward the table where her breakfast awaited her.

Abigail stared after her. Who had won the first round? Probably neither. When Michal learned that Abigail—not she—would share David's bed tonight, she might well be provoked to a furious outburst. This day could well mark the end of the happiness and tranquillity of the royal family.

David returned to the house in the late afternoon. Tonight he had no guests for supper, although his wives as usual had prepared for more. Only Shammah and Hezro shared the meal on the rooftop that evening. Shortly after eating, the two warriors retired with their wives to their own private sleeping rooms on the rooftop.

David stood alone by the parapet, facing the west, watching the fading colors of the dying sunset and enjoying the evening breeze. The women had already cleared away the remains of the supper.

"Abigail." He spoke softly, without taking his eyes off the distant horizon.

Abigail heard his word, and came to him. "Yes, my lord husband?"

"The festivities last night were handled well, my love."

"Thank you."

It was unlike him to compliment her for doing what she was only expected to do. She searched for a deeper meaning in his words. She thought she found it, and his next few statements confirmed this.

"You handle all the duties of first wife with great competence. In every area."

"Thank you."

"Including the management of a growing number of wives."

She waited, knowing he would have more to say.

122

He sighed. "I'm sorry I pushed the burden of a new wife on your shoulders at a difficult time for you, the burden of a wife filled to overflowing with pride and bitterness."

Abigail smiled in the darkness. He understood more than a man should. He had been preoccupied with matters of state last night, but he had been sensitive enough to be aware of the domestic problem in his household.

He turned to her now, a sad smile on his face. "Is everything all right, my love?"

She smiled at him and steadied her voice to reflect assurance and calmness. "Of course, my husband. Don't worry. Everything is under control in your family."

He studied her face a moment, and his thumb and forefinger went unconsciously to his chin. Abigail began to feel uneasy under his scrutiny.

"I hope you understand why I took her back," he said softly. He referred to Michal, of course.

She nodded.

"She is the daughter of King Saul. You wanted to show everyone that the House of David retains its ties with the House of Saul."

"You always grasp the political situation—better than most men. Yes, that's the main reason. But . . . there is another."

Abigail waited. She sensed her husband had something he felt he needed to say to her.

He continued. "I want everyone to know that the household of the king is protected. I don't want anyone to take you away from me. Whether Amalekites or . . . an individual." He paused. "Do you understand what I'm saying?" His words were ambiguous. He could refer to the entire retinue of wives, a protection extended to the entire king's family. This, she knew, was a policy established by all kings everywhere.

He had referred to his rescue of his family from the Amalekites. It would have been much simpler merely to take a few new wives and begin again. But he hadn't done that. To establish firmly the principle that the royal family was inviolate?

Or could he mean . . . just her? His true love?

She smiled. It was foolish, she knew, but she decided to accept the latter meaning. "Thank you, my love," she murmured.

He stood there in the starlight, looking tenderly down on her. Yes, she could easily believe that second meaning. She pushed out of her mind the thought that he might well say the same thing to each of his wives. No. That could not be. He had meant it about her. Her alone.

His next words were an invitation, but not a command. "Would you like to tell me what happened last night?"

Abigail paused. She had promised herself to handle the domestic problem alone, without her husband's intervention. She would still do that, but why not tell him? He might even be amused, but she knew he would not interfere.

So she told him. She began with Shua's near-hysterical report of the chaos below during the serving of the meal, and what she had found when the evening's work was completed. She portrayed Michal's grand entrance this morning in the courtyard, and a word-for-word description of their confrontation.

Through it all, David chuckled softly. As Abigail suspected, he enjoyed the tale immensely. When she had finished he turned his face toward her and grinned. "I thought it was something like that," he said softly. "Also, I had confidence in your ability to handle the situation. I see my confidence was not misplaced."

"*My* confidence was bolstered by your invitation to me to spend the night with you, my husband."

"I confess that one reason I extended that invitation was to assure you of my support. But there was another reason.

"Oh?"

He reached over and touched her hand. "I have missed you in my bed, my love. While I am doing my duty as a king with my wives, I think of you often. It has been so long."

Her heart leaped within her. Nothing he could have said would have warmed her more than those words.

"Thank you, my love. I have missed you also."

"Then we must waste no more time out here. Come, let us go—"

He broke off, as the noise of a disturbance reached them coming from the courtyard below. Voices. Angry voices. Michal again? No. Those were men's voices.

David strode across the roof to the parapet overlooking the courtyard. Abigail followed.

"Joab!" The word burst from David's lips.

The scene which greeted Abigail in the courtyard was ghostly and nightmarish. Two men stood below, holding torches which flickered on their helmets and cast dancing shadows on the ground around them.

Joab. And his brother Abishai.

18

"WHAT HAVE YOU done?" Joab shouted the question, his words sharp and angry. "You let our enemy get away, and you had him right here—"

"Joab, calm down. I'll explain—"

"Don't you know that Abner is our enemy? Don't you know that even now he's plotting treachery against you? He came here to spy on you. In a few weeks he'll be back with an army to destroy you."

"Joab. Listen to me. He—"

But Joab wouldn't listen. He turned and strode out the courtyard gate, his brother following. Darkness suddenly engulfed the courtyard, and Abigail could see the two torches moving jerkily through the city in the direction of Joab's house.

In the pale starlight, Abigail could see the hard set of David's face. "Why do you let him speak to you like that?" she asked gently.

He shook his head sadly. "He's my nephew. Never have I questioned his loyalty. He's a man of explosive temper. He didn't mean to insult me."

"But . . . what will he do?"

David shrugged. "Nothing, probably. Let's wait and see. After his temper subsides, he'll accept the situation."

"But if he doesn't? What if he decides to take matters

into his own hands? He's done it before."

David turned to her and smiled. "It's in Yahweh's hands, my love. Let's leave it there."

Abigail felt herself stiffening at these words. Always her husband took refuge in piety. Sincere piety, to be sure, but sometimes David's faith refused to accept reality. Let Yahweh do it all. Let the kingdom fall in ruins and do nothing to prevent it—if it was Yahweh's will. Too much piety could well lead to his own destruction.

But she couldn't say that to him. Instead she asked, "What will you do?"

"Whatever I do, I'll do it tomorrow. Not tonight. We have more important matters ahead of us tonight."

He took her hand and led her to his sleeping room.

But the spell was gone. That magical love-moment had been shattered by Joab's savage entrance. She wondered if they could ever recover it.

Yet they did. In David's arms, surrounded by his assurances of his love for her, she found peace. Forgotten was the sight of an angry Joab with his brother in the torchlit courtyard and the sinister words which followed.

All she wanted to remember was the blissful part of the night, and her beloved's tender assurances of his love.

The next day, shortly after sunrise, David left the house to seek out Joab. "To make amends," he told Abigail.

Midway through the morning she sensed an excitement in the city. When the courtyard gates were opened to the venders, she learned the news.

"Abner is dead," one merchant told her.

"Joab killed him," another said.

But they could tell her no more. It was too early. The news was so fresh details were not yet known.

The beggars would know. They seemed to know everything that happened in Hebron. She would talk to them when she fed them at noon.

The usual crowd had gathered outside the gate of her house where they knew she would bring to them scraps from last night's supper and this morning's breakfast. Abigail recognized two of them: Shecaniah the Ithrite and Arnan the Shumathite, two old soldiers who had fought in Saul's army in the early days. They had left Saul to follow David. Both came from ancient Hebronite families, but old age and infirmity had reduced them to poverty. They were regulars at David's gate.

They were full of the news. Abigail did not have to pump them for it.

Shecaniah's bony fingers crammed stale bread into his toothless mouth. Because of that, his words came out garbled. "That Joab, he smart. He kill old man Abner."

Arnan had leaned his crutch on the wall to free both his hands to hold the cheese he was attacking.

"Stuck him right in the gizzard, he did. Hee, hee. Just like the old man did to Asahel."

He referred to the young brother of Joab, whom Abner had killed a few years ago. Joab and Abishai had sworn a blood oath to avenge their brother's death.

"Where did it happen?" asked Abigail.

"City gate, mum," replied Shecaniah.

"But Abner left yesterday. How. . . ?"

"Dunno." Arnan leaned against the wall. His twisted leg would not support him. "He must have sent him a message. Hah! Bait, most likely. Told him the king wanted to see him, and to get him back here now!"

"You shouldda seen your husband the king, mum, when he found out. Tore his robe. Dirtied himself with dust. Wailed. Loud, too. Made sure them big hogs from the tribes of Israel heard him."

"Don't kid yourself, Shec." Arnan shoved bread and cheese into the pouch of his ragged clothes. "The king meant it. He wasn't faking. Didn't you see them tears?"

"Yeah, well, maybe so. But Joab didn't mean nothing, and he wailed just as loud as the king!"

Abigail stiffened. Yes, her husband would mourn sincerely the loss of Abner. He would do so for more than just political reasons; she knew David had truly loved and respected his old enemy.

But Joab? His grief was hypocritical. David should have punished Joab, not allowed him to bemoan the passing of the man he had just killed. Politics again. Joab knew the ambassadors were watching. By joining in the grief, he would convey an impression to them—of what? They would know his sorrow was not sincere. Then why. . . ?

She shook her head, bewildered, and listened to more of the gossip from the street-wise beggars.

"Old Joab—he know what he's doing. He know them big hogs from Israel would think he stuck Abner because of the blood vengeance. They won't blame it on the king. Hee, hee. Just a private feud."

"But in Hebron? The City of Refuge?" asked Abigail.

"Don't mean nothin' to Joab, mum," replied Shecaniah. "He got no scruples, like your husband."

"Blood feud, that was only part of it." Arnan shoved a piece of cheese into his pouch. "Old Abner, he gonna be commander-in-chief. Joab, he didn't like that—not at all."

"Where are they now?" asked Abigail.

Shecaniah too was secreting bread and cheese in his clothes. He replied, "Burying Abner. That funeral procession went toward the Wall of the Tombs."

The Wall of the Tombs—the rocky hillside to the east where the wealthy people of Hebron owned sepulchers. Then David was giving Abner an honorable funeral and interment. To impress the ambassadors of Israel of his innocence? Yes, he would do that. But David would do it also to honor Abner. Meanwhile Joab would be beside him, wailing loud as anybody. The politics of grief.

As she left the two old soldiers to return to her household chores, she knew she would not need to prepare supper tonight. David would be fasting, as he always did when his men were slain in battle.

Then a chilling thought struck her. Those beggars. They had been cramming food into their clothes. Streetwise, they had guessed even before Abigail that there would be no supper tonight in the royal household and thus no food scraps for charity tomorrow. Fasting at a funeral meant nothing to them, as it did to David.

Again she marveled at her husband. He was not only a devout man but also a shrewd politician. He kept the two qualities balanced in his personality. His grief for Abner was both heartfelt and practical—at the same time.

Joab had violated the law by killing his blood enemy in a City of Refuge. He had clearly defied the express command of his king. He deserved death. And yet he lived. He retained his post as commander-in-chief. He mourned loudly at the funeral of his hated enemy.

David would do nothing about it. He needed Joab. He needed a bloody hatchet-man, who would do what needed to be done without remorse, without conscience, without hesitation.

David could not do those things. David was gentle, sensitive, deeply religious. It was not in his nature.

But he knew—knew with the canniness of a shrewd politician—that these things had to be done. And so he kept Joab by his side.

"He's my nephew," had been his simple answer to the question she had put to him just last night. "Never have I questioned his loyalty."

Abigail sighed. Yes, her husband needed Joab. David knew it; so did Joab. How many more such incidents lay ahead?

19

MAACAH, THE PROUD young princess from Geshur, solved the problem of Michal's takeover of the sleeping room. One day when Michal left the room to march regally toward the breakfast table, Maacah picked up her infant son and with her three servants marched into the room with their bedding and possessions. When Michal returned, she found them busy rearranging furniture and settling in.

It was done so suddenly, every one—the wives included—were caught by surprise. Abigail fully expected an outraged outburst from Michal, but there was none. Instead she merely shrugged and accepted the inevitable.

Before the day was over, many of the other women had also moved in. Michal made no objection. Although she still held herself aloof from the other wives, she caused no more trouble.

Occasionally Michal turned her sharp tongue on one or another of the women or children with whom she shared the crowded house. Following the example set by Abigail, each outburst was either ignored or met with a cheerful response.

Ahinoam recalled an old proverb which soon came to everyone's lips as they shared an inside joke. "A soft answer turns away wrath, but harsh words stir up anger." And Abigail herself recalled another proverb, much to everyone's delight. "It is better to live in a corner of the rooftop, than in a grand house with a contentious wife."

A curious friendship developed between Michal and Maacah. Abigail watched in amazement as the bond between the two women increased. They had so little in common, other than both having been born in a royal household. There was the age difference—fifteen years separated them. Michal was childless, while Maacah nursed an infant son. David occasionally invited Maacah to his bed, but ignored Michal. Michal had come to the household with no servants, while Maacah was attended by three serving girls from her home country. The older woman displayed outbursts of an ugly temper. She remained haughty and detached, while the younger, since accepting Abigail's leadership in the household, was cheerful and popular, with many friends. Yet in spite of their differences, the two were drawn to each other, and as a result the level of tension lowered in the royal household.

David became aware of the harmony in his family, and spoke of it once to Abigail as they talked on the rooftop at night. "Michal seems to have accepted her place?" It was a question, not a statement, inviting an explanation.

Abigail shrugged. "She seems so lonely. She needed someone, and somehow Maacah happened to be the one she reached out for."

"A strange match."

"Yes." Abigail paused, wondering whether the question she wanted to ask would offend her husband. She decided to ask it anyway."I think, my husband, that . . . she still loves you. If you would take her to your bed—just once—it might sweeten her disposition a little."

David's face seemed to set into hard lines. "No. It is enough that I took her into my household. But I will not sire any children through her."

He gave no further explanation, and Abigail did not

press him. But by his words, he had sentenced Michal to a life of loneliness. Abigail searched the face of her husband, whom she had thought she understood. This man, thoughtful and sensitive to his wives, turned his back on Michal. He had snatched her from the arms of a man who worshiped her, from a household where she was mistress of the house, held in honor by all, and shoved her brutally into a small corner where she had neither power nor friends to sustain her.

And then—he refused to give her his love. Abigail looked at her husband, wondering at his complicated nature.

David had always been an unfailing well of love. He always displayed tender passion for each of his wives. As each one entered his life, his warm personal affection reached out and included her. Abigail recalled how David always made her feel that she—and she only—was his true love. Did he make each of his wives feel the same?

Probably. He had that ability. But why was she herself not jealous? Why did she not turn into a shrew—like Michal—and make all her rivals miserable? What was there about her husband that enabled her to accept a sharing of his affection, rather than demanding that it be given exclusively to her?

David was an enigma, deep and complicated. He married for political or financial reasons, but loved each wife individually. This should cause jealousy among the women who lived with him, but it actually accomplished the opposite: they adored him. Even Michal. Of all people, Michal should hate him. But she didn't. She still clung to the infatuation she had for him in her youth. But because he rebuffed her, she turned her hatred on others. Michal was the only one in the household of royal consorts who was shrewish and spiteful.

Abigail always smiled to herself as she thought about

her unfathomable husband. If anyone had the basic natural ability to assume the throne of Israel, develop the nation into one of the earth's great powers, and establish a dynasty that would last forever, it was he. Surely God had touched his life. Surely David would be the chief instrument in the hands of Yahweh to fulfill the ancient promise.

Then, one quiet evening, an event occurred which made the fulfillment of that promise a little more possible.

The men sat at supper on the rooftop. The sunset heralded the breeze which made these evening meals a delight for the men and an opportunity to relax from their day's work. On this evening David had no foreign dignitaries as his guest. Instead he was hosting several of his Mighty Men.

Supper was finished, and the men sat lazily with their wine cups, enjoying the encroaching darkness and the cooling breeze. David reached for his lyre, and the men hushed their talk and turned to him.

Just as his fingers strummed the first note, they were distracted by a disturbance below. The guards at the courtyard gate had challenged someone who loudly demanded permission to see the king.

Shammah, seated nearest the parapet overlooking the courtyard, rose and looked down.

"Two men," he reported. He squinted into the darkness. "I think I recognize them."

"Who are they?" asked David.

"Rechab and Baanah. They are Benjaminites. Former officers in Saul's army."

David nodded. "I remember them. Abner's lieutenants. Now they serve Ishbosheth. Are they armed?"

Shammah shook his head. "No. But one of them is carrying a sack. I don't think it's a weapon."

"Then let them come up. We'll see what they have to say."

A moment later the two men topped the stairway and stood at the end of the large banquet table facing David. The sack one of them carried had a round object in it.

"My lord king," said one triumphantly. "We bring you great news. Your last enemy is dead!"

"What do you mean?" demanded David.

The man with the sack placed it on the table. He reached into it and brought forth the round object.

A human head!

Abigail felt her stomach churn. The head was several days old. She could smell the putrid odor from her corner of the rooftop. The features had been distorted and blackened.

"Behold!" shouted the man, as he held the grisly object by the hair and lifted it high. "The head of Ishbosheth, son of your enemy Saul, who sought your life! On this day, Yahweh has given you the final victory against all your enemies!"

David's men rose to their feet. They stared at the severed head. Torchlight flickered on the features, which seemed to leer at the company of men.

David too rose. He spoke sharply.

"Who killed him?" he demanded.

"We did, my lord king. May all your enemies perish as this one did!"

The other man now spoke. He poured out a passionate story of how they had sneaked into the king's house in Mahanaim, where they assassinated Ishbosheth while he lay on his bed taking a midday nap.

David waited patiently until the story was finished. Then his voice lashed out like an iron sword. "I swear by Yahweh—who alone delivers me from my enemies—that when someone tells me he has slain Yahweh's anointed king, that man must die! Thus has it always been, and *thus it is now!*"

He nodded to Shammah, who grasped the arm of the man who held the head in his hand. Others of David's soldiers leaped forward, making the two men prisoners.

"Take them away!" shouted David. "By tomorrow morning, when the people of Hebron come to the pool to gather water, I want them to find the bodies of these traitors hanging by the tree, with their hands and feet severed! This is the fate of anyone who harms the family of Yahweh's Anointed!'

"But . . . but my lord David—"

Their protests were cut short as David's men hustled the two Benjaminites down the stairs and out through the courtyard gate.

When they had gone, David spoke softly. "This head." His word drew the attention of the remaining warriors to the horrid object on the table before them. "Tomorrow, this head will receive an honorable burial. In the tomb of Abner. And we shall fast and mourn his death. So let it be."

Abigail shuddered. The ghastly event had left her shaken and moved. Even so, she knew that what her husband had done was an act of statesmanship which once again proved his worthiness to be the Anointed of Yahweh. All Israel would know that he had nothing to do with the death of the last remnant of the House of Saul.

And now nothing stood in the way of his becoming king of all Israel.

20

THE DAYS passed. The people of the household went about their work with laughter and harmony. The *yoreh* arrived—the first rain of the season. Now the days turned cold and blustery. The evening suppers, often formal occasions with important guests, were held in one of the rooms opening onto the courtyard. The cooking took place outside, while the men gathered in the brazier-warmed room and feasted.

Abigail, who supervised these important banquets, made sure she stayed in the room where the men were served and entertained. She wanted to see the dignitaries who shared David's table—and to hear their discussions.

As the Israelites assembled in Hebron for the coronation, many delegations from all the tribes camped outside the city. David issued as many daily invitations as the banquet room would seat. And so Abigail saw them all. She saw the ancient elders, their proud beards long and oiled; the young military captains, often wearing ceremonial swords; the wealthy landowners, dressed in fine well-tailored clothes; the scribes, the priests, the prophets, the sages. They had come from every tribe, "from Dan to Beer-sheba." Many came because of curiosity, to see this talented youth who would soon be their king. Some were former enemies who had served in King Saul's army. Most were friendly, a few reserved, but none openly hostile.

David discussed with them the terms of his reign. They would all support him with a standing army. The size of their military contribution would depend on the size of the tribe and their ability to furnish young trained fighting men. They would also offer wealth, including sheep and goats and cattle and donkeys and even some camels and horses. Occasionally David demanded gold and silver, depending on their ability to pay. These taxes, David told them, were mostly to support the standing army.

David himself contracted to defend the nation from all enemies, be the final judge of appeals on rulings in matters of civil and criminal justice, protect travelers, encourage foreign trade, and send ambassadors to the nations surrounding them. And most important: to maintain a royal court to rival any court in the world, that this nation—Israel—might hold its head high in the community of nations.

David charmed the ambassadors from the tribes. He told them intimate stories about himself, not boastful but homey and endearing. He listened to them, listened thoughtfully and with personal attention, making promises he felt he could keep, giving understanding and sympathy when he could not help.

And he sang for them. The men of Israel learned once again why, as a youth in King Saul's court, he had earned the name "Sweet Singer of Israel."

Abigail continued to marvel at David's natural ability to assume the appearance of kingship. He looked like a king. He spoke like a king. He conducted his business and political affairs like a king. No ruler in any court—Egypt, Babylon, Syria, or those rumored fabled lands across the Great Sea—could possibly be more regal than the man who would soon be anointed king of Israel.

Not only did delegations come from the tribes of Israel but also from other nations. Abigail was particularly impressed with Hiram, a young prince from the Phoenician port of Tyre. He wore the purple robe which was the trademark of his country, and wherever Phoenician ships traveled on the Great Sea, the "Nation of Purple Cloth" was known.

Hiram, although very young, showed signs of maturity and intelligence as he faced David across the banquet table as an equal. "My father offers you his friendship," he said cordially. "As do I."

"His friendship is valued," replied David. "And returned—for both father and son."

"The great king of Israel should dwell in a splendid palace," the youth observed. "Do you plan to build one?"

"Soon. But first I would build a temple to the glory of Yahweh. I cannot live in a magnificent house while my God lives in a tent."

"Then I know you will build both, great king. And my country will furnish the wood and the craftsmen for these buildings."

Abigail knew—as did everyone everywhere—that the second world-famous product of this small but powerful nation was wood. Wood from the famous cedars of Lebanon. Not only were the Phoenicians known and respected on the sea, but also on land—as builders. Tyre, their capitol city, boasted some of the finest construction in the world. Their wood structures rivaled in beauty and solidity the magnificent architecture of Thebes, whose building material was massive blocks of polished stone.

David smiled in his charming way. "And I will pay you full value for your materials and skill."

Hiram waved a hand and smiled, revealing his own charm. "Let there be no talk of pay. No contract need exist between us. Only friendship. Our gifts to you will bear no price."

"Nor will our gifts to you," replied David.

Two kings faced each other. Two kings who had yet to be crowned in their kingdoms. One would be crowned within the month. The other, on the death of his father. And, Abigail hoped, the friendship between the kings would endure for generations.

21

THE DAY ARRIVED for the coronation. No wind blew that day, but the air was bitterly cold. Occasional rain squalls added chilling fingers to the occasion. The dark sky glowered down on the vast company gathered in the pasture, as though to presage ominous times for the new king.

The ceremony had to be held outside. No single building could hold them all, and to exclude anyone would be an unforgivable insult. David's wives watched in shivering awe from the rooftop of the royal house as the assembly in the pasture outside the city proceeded to crown the popular young king.

David had set the tone of the coronation by using his own priest, Abiathar. In doing so, he proclaimed to all that he—not the dignitaries from the other tribes—was in charge.

This would be his third anointing. The first had been by the legendary prophet Samuel, in another pasture near Bethlehem. The second was here, on this same spot, when David was crowned king of Judah. Now a priest of Judah poured a vial of olive oil on David's head, proclaiming him the divinely appointed king of all Israel. Thus he sent a message to all that here was Yahweh's Anointed One. He would rule in his own way, with his own people in high positions, and everyone must obey.

Abigail, clutching her woolen cloak around her, was too far away to hear the ceremony, but she watched as the tribes came forward to kneel before their king and pledge loyalty and support. Abiathar himself slit the throats of the twelve bullocks for the ritual sacrifice and lit the fires to burn the bullocks as a thank offering to Yahweh. Soon the fires lifted white fingers of smoke to the gray skies as the ceremony at last came to an end.

The women on the rooftop scurried below to the brazier warmed rooms, but Abigail remained, comfortable in her warm cloak, thoughtfully watching the assembly disburse.

So . . . Israel had a new king. Her husband. He had come a long way since he first walked into her life.

She smiled, recalling how her first impression of him had been so wrong. A savage, she thought then. An outlaw, a renegade, in open rebellion against Yahweh's Anointed. Now . . . now she understood him as clearly as anyone in Israel could understand this enigmatic young king.

He had been chosen and prepared by Yahweh as part of the promise given to their ancestor Abraham. The nation God had selected as his own would be large and powerful, and through them all nations would be blessed. David—her husband—was an important part of that promise.

The dynasty established this day seemed permanent and secure. For how long? David's lifetime? The lifetime of his sons? Twenty centuries?

Or . . . forever?

She shrugged. She turned to go below. Such matters were in the hand of Yahweh. It was enough to be a small part of them.

Author's Footnote

THE STORY of King David's life is only half-finished. Many more adventures lie ahead, some exciting, some successful, some tragic—all colorful. These stories will be told in the next People of the Promise book, *Bathsheba* (Herald Press, 1996).

Author

JAMES R. SHOTT insists that he did not retire from the Presbyterian ministry in 1980; he merely changed directions. Now the focus of his ministry is the written rather than the preached word.

Shott has had many articles, poems, short stories, and sermons as well as a children's novel published. He delights in speaking to children's groups at schools and churches.

His Herald Press series, The People of the Promise (*Leah, Hagar, Joseph, Esau, Deborah, Othniel, Abigail*), brings to life the men and women of the Old Testament who lived by God's promise: "Through you, all the families of the earth shall be blessed."

Shott attends First Presbyterian Church in Palm Bay, Florida, where he lives with his wife, Esther B. Shott.